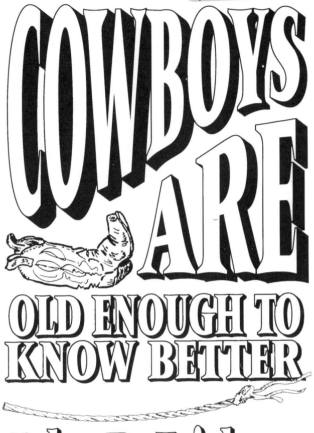

COWBOYS ARE
OLD ENOUGH TO KNOW BETTER

John R. Erickson
Illustrated by Gerald L. Holmes

Maverick Books
Published by Gulf Publishing Company
Houston, Texas

Maverick Books
Published by Gulf Publishing Company
P. O. Box 2608, Houston, Texas 77252-2608

10 9 8 7 6 5 4 3 2

Printed in the United States of America.

Library of Congress Cataloging-in-Publication Data

Erickson, John R., 1943–
    Cowboys are old enough to know better/John R. Erickson: illustrated by Gerald L. Holmes.
        p.   cm.
    ISBN 0-87719-256-1
        1. Cowboys—West (U.S.)—Fiction. 2. Ranch life—West (U.S.)—Fiction. I. Title
PS3555.R428C595 1994
813'.54—dc20   94-32156
                                                        CIP

Contents

Chapter One
Sue 'em!

The other day I stopped in to see Willie Onthenextranch. He was guarding the coffee pot and I figured he might need some help.

He claims that if you don't watch that pot real close on a cold day, it'll go to whistling and popping and spook the cattle in the home pasture.

He'd been reading the paper before I got there, and he showed me a story on the front page. It told about a feller in California who tried to murder his mother-in-law with a scoop shovel.

He didn't get the job done, and he got sent to the pen for trying. While he was in the pen, he hired a lawyer and sued his mother-in-law for making him mad enough to want to kill her.

He won. The judge said it was her fault.

Well, the story went on, if it was her fault, then what was *he* doing in the pen? He sued the judge and the jury that had sent him up, and he won that one too. Then he sued the state and the newspapers, and he won again.

This being California, they finally got everything straightened out. They sent the mother-in-law to the pen after she got out of the hospital, and old Scoop Shovel collected a million dollars in damages.

1

This fall, he was elected to Congress and now he wants to serve on the House Ethics Committee.

Well, the story burned me up and I raved for fifteen minutes about how there ought to be a law against that kind of law. Willie just listened and grinned, and I asked him what the heck was wrong with him.

"There's a lesson here for the cowman," he said. "No wonder we ain't making any money in the cattle business."

I asked just what he meant by that.

He ran a toothpick through his uppers. "Listen, we're wasting our money on high-powered bulls and herd improvement. We don't need better cattle. We need better *lawyers*."

I didn't know what to say, so I let him go on.

"Now, you take that Beef Boycott in 1973. Instead of talking to those people, we should have sued 'em for corrupting our livelihood. And when the calf market busted in '74, we should have sued the buyers.

"When gas and cottonseed cake and pickups and steel went up, we should have sued the manufacturers. Every time the truckers and meat cutters got a raise in pay, we should have sued the unions. And you remember that big blizzard in '71? The Weather Bureau didn't predict it, so we should have sued them too."

Old Willie rubbed his hands together and flashed a smile full of poison. "Yalp, I've got it figgered. The way to make money in this day and time is to hire good lawyers, raise sorry cattle, and sue anybody who don't like it."

"It won't work," I said. "It's a supply and demand market. If the consumer won't pay . . ."

"Then we'll meet 'em at the courthouse! What right does the consumer have not to buy our beef? And if they get snuffy, we'll have 'em throwed in jail."

"A hundred million consumers?"

"It'll take a few lawyers, but it can be done."

"When all the consumers are in jail, who's going to buy beef?"

Willie shrugged. "Then we'll sue the police. Sue the prison wardens. Sue the government!"

"We ARE the government, Willie. You'd be suing yourself." I got up to leave. "Which ain't a bad idea. You ought to sue yourself for being dumb enough to get into the cow business in the first place."

He rubbed his chin. "I never thought of that. You know, if a guy had a real sharp lawyer and put his ranch into a corporation . . ."

I slammed the door and went home. Sometimes I think the Founding Fathers were too optimistic about human nature. Our form of government would be great if it weren't for all the people.

Chapter Two
Willie's Mileage Log

I'd finished my daily feed run. It was too early to go to the house but too late to start any kind of major project.

And besides, it was too derned cold. Radio said the chill factor was down around 20 below. The only heater in my barn is the pair of long johns you wear into it.

I baled up a few gunny sacks until my feet got numb. Then I scooped up some of the cake the pack rats had scattered. Then I got the axe out of the corner and went out to the big stock tank in front of the barn.

Thought I might as well chop out my Christmas tree.

I had taken a few swings at the ice when I heard a rattling noise. I looked around and saw an old red four-wheel drive turn in and cross the cattle guard.

It was Willie Onthenextranch.

I hurried away from the stock tank and went back to the barn, hoping he wouldn't notice what I'd been doing. He did, of course. He has a genius for finding every little mistake. He slowed down, craned his neck, and squinted at the stock tank.

He got out and walked over to where I was. His first four steps would have made you think he was an invalid, but after that he got his joints oiled up.

"Pretty cold," he said.

"Yup."

"Likely to get colder tonight."

"Yup."

"Radio says we might get snow."

"Yup."

"If you can believe the danged radio."

"Yup."

"Which you can't."

"Nope."

He flicked out one finger toward the tank. "What you got in there?"

"Oh, that's where we're storing our ice this winter."

"What's that green thing?"

"Green ice. We use it for special occasions."

"Very funny." He walked over to the tank and I followed. He studied the tree for about half a minute, then, "Well, you sure screwed that deal up, didn't you?"

"I wouldn't put it exactly that way."

"Shall I guess? You bought a Christmas tree around the fifteenth of December. Weather was open, pretty warm. You got home and noticed that the needles were falling off the tree. Am I right?"

"Maybe."

"Tree was dried out. So instead of standing it up in a bucket of water, which would have required a little labor on your part, you just pitched the son of a buck into the tank." His eyes were sparkling now. "Only you hadn't counted on that big norther blowing in the next day and dropping the temperature down to three below zero."

"It was only two below."

"And so you learned a valuable lesson about cutting corners and ended up with your Christmas tree frozen into about five tons of solid ice."

"I doubt if it weighs that much."

"And you had to go to town and buy another one."

"Yeah, but they were on sale by then."

He grinned. "And you didn't want me to know about it, did you? Thought you could run over here to the barn and I wouldn't pay any attention. Heh, heh. But you got caught."

"That's a very narrow way of looking at it."

"The truth," he said, poking me in the chest with his finger, "is always narrow. You might try to remember that." He started back to his pickup. "Well, I can't stand around here all day listening to you yap."

"*Me* yap!"

"I've got work to do."

"What work do you have to do? You've fed your cows and you don't have many chores."

He didn't answer, but opened his pickup door and picked something off the dash. He held it up. It was a small cassette tape recorder. He pressed a button and spoke into the built-in microphone.

"It is now 4:32 P.M., January 20 in the year of our Lord 1985, and mileage on the old red pickup stands at 97,365.4. I drove four and four-tenths miles from the bull pasture to my neighbor's place. During that time my wheels turned 4,329 times, my pistons chugged 13,509 times, my fan made 53,596 revolutions, and I burned up approximately 3 quarts of tax-exempt agricultural gasoline."

"What are you doing?"

He snapped off the machine. "Being a good tax-paying citizen, what do think? Don't tell me you're not filling out your mileage log."

"Well, to tell you the truth . . ."

"Just as I suspected! Disobeying the law of the land."

"Willie, it's a crazy law. There's no way we can keep up with every trip, every stop, every mile."

"Sure you can. Get you one of these tape recorders, talk into it as you go, keep good records. It ain't so bad, and it's the least we can do for our friends at the Internal Revenue Service."

I studied his face. He shaved with an electric razor and he'd missed a little circle of whiskers on his left cheek. "Willie, this doesn't sound like you. I would have expected you to go through the ceiling when your accountant gave you the news about this mileage log."

"Me? That would be childish and immature."

"Right. That's what I mean."

He shook his head. "I'm beyond that. I've decided to cooperate, be a good citizen. I mean, this is *tax reform*, ain't it?" He snapped on the machine. "Let's see, I'm holding a business conference here with my neighbor. What's your social security number?" I gave it to him and he went on. "This is a very important, high-level executive management conference. Subject: a mysterious tree found growing in my neighbor's stock tank in the middle of January."

"Oh. I'm beginning to get it."

Willie snapped off the machine and raised one eyebrow just a tad. "They want to know what I'm doing? They're fixing to find out, every detail. Soon as I leave here, I'm going home and me and Iris will spend four hours typing the stuff up. Already got two boot boxes full. Another week and we'll have three.

"Then we'll ship 'em to the IRS in Austin, and I'm sending along these instructions. Here, look 'em over." He reached into the pickup and brought out a sheet of paper with typing on it. Here's what it said:

"Dear IRS Friend:

"Enclosed you will find my vehicle mileage log for the month of January 1985. Say, I had a ball with this thing. The more I wrote down, the more I wanted to write.

"Gets kind of boring on the feed run, see, just me and the old cows, and this mileage log has really filled a void. I think February's log is going to be even longer, more detailed, and better. I hope you enjoy it, 'cause I went to a lot of trouble to do it.

"Which brings me to the point of this letter. I went to so much trouble working on my mileage log, I would be real disappointed if nobody at the IRS bothered to read it. If you don't mind, I'd like for you guys to keep a log too. Nothing elaborate or complicated.

Just have the reader keep his time. Oh, and don't forget to put down a Social Security number.

"Any time the reader looks away from the text, we'll want that information. This includes lunch breaks and coffee breaks, trips to the water cooler, pencil sharpener, garbage can, and bathroom; all forms of coughing, napping on the job, goofing off, and looking at persons of the opposite sex.

"Again, nothing complicated. Just the year, month, day, hour, minute, and second.

"Should the reader speak to anyone during the reading of my log, I would like Social Security numbers, automobile serial numbers, and shoe sizes of all persons spoken to. Also a list of movies they saw in 1984.

"Sneezing is exempt IF the reader can produce proof of allergy. 'Proof' shall consist of letters from three doctors and one mother, as well as three used Kleenexes.

"Please submit your log of my log in an original and three copies. Deadline shall be thirty days after my log reaches your office. Failure to keep these records will lead to grave consequences: GOD WILL GET YOU."

I looked up and saw a smirk on Willie's mouth. "You wouldn't actually send this off, would you?"

"Why not? I'm a taxpaying citizen. I got my rights. By netties, if they can demand records of us, we can demand records right back."

"Yes Willie, but . . ."

"And let me tell you something, pardner." He squinted one eye and sighted down his finger-pistol. "If a couple thousand of us cowboys send in our mileage logs in boot-box lots, them beerocrats are gonna get tired of us real fast."

He climbed into his pickup and slammed the door and leaned his face out the window. "And you thought I wouldn't see your Christmas tree in the ice. Heh. You got to get up pretty early in the morning to fool old Willie." He winked at me. "Just ask the IRS."

G. L. Holmes

He fired up his pickup. When the first cloud of blue smoke floated past and I dared breathe again, I hollered at him as he was backing out. "Hey Willie, may I ask you a personal question?"

His eyes narrowed. "Maybe. But only one. I'm a very busy man."

"Did you think you had a cassette in that tape recorder?"

His brows twitched ever so slightly. His hand shot down to the seat and brought up the recorder. He flipped it open. It was empty. His eyes came up and the blue veins stood out on his forehead.

"You always did have a smart alecky streak."

"I won't tell about your tape recorder if you won't tell about my Christmas tree."

"Okay, but there's a difference between my mistake and your mistake."

"Oh?"

"Yours was dumb and mine was honest. Goodbye and drop dead."

And with that, he roared off.

Chapter Three

Willie's Lawn Mower

It was Wednesday morning and I'd made arrangements to pick up Willie Onthenextranch. Wednesday was our big day. We were going into to town to the livestock auction.

I pulled up in front of his place around ten. We usually tried to go early, have a piece of pie and a cup of coffee, talk around with the farmers and ranchers about moisture and grass and such important stuff, and make it into the sale barn in time for the jackpot sale at eleven.

We rarely bought anything. Every now and then one of us would pick up a baby calf to adopt on a first-calf heifer or we might pick up a saddle at the right price. But mainly we went to the sale because it was the big social event of the week.

I got out of my pickup, kicked Willie's two dogs out of the way, stumbled over a cat and three kittens, and went toward the front door. I heard a lawn mower running on the west side of the house, so I peeked around the corner.

I couldn't believe my eyes. Willie was mowing the grass, and it couldn't have been more than four inches tall! Usually he waited until it was about right for a swather.

When he saw me standing there, he hit the kill switch and walked toward me, mopping his red face with a red bandanna. "Took your sweet time about getting here, didn't you?"

"It's ten o'clock. I said I'd be here at ten."

"That's fine for you, but what about me? Iris stuck me on that danged mowing machine. If you'd come half an hour early, I could have quit, but you don't care about your friends. You never think of anyone but yourself. Let's get out of here."

We headed for the pickup. "Willie, if it makes you feel any better, the yard looks nice — what you mowed of it."

He got in and slammed his door and slid his eyes in my direction. "It don't make me feel any better. What would make me feel better would be three loads of gravel spread over that yard. Do you remember how to drive this thing?"

"What thing?"

"This pickup. I'd like to get to the sale before it's over."

"Oh. Well, let me see here." I hit the starter, put her in gear, and pulled away from the house. We headed down the road toward town. The third cattle guard between Willie's place and the highway was pretty rough, and when we hit it, a bunch of miller moths came out of the heater vents and fell down from the sun visors.

In our country, May is National Miller Moth Month. All at once, and for no reason that I know of, millers are everywhere. For a couple of weeks they hide under your saddle blankets and bed sheets and take up residence in your boots and always seem to find their way into your first cup of coffee. Then in June they disappear, thank goodness.

Willie stared at the fifteen millers that were flying in crazy circles against the windshield. "That's got to be the most worthless creature on this earth. They have wings but they can't even fly in a straight line." We drove on, both of us looking out at the pastures and trying to keep the millers from flying down the necks of our shirts.

"Grass sure looks good, doesn't it?" I said.

That was the wrong thing to say. "It does unless you have to mow the danged hateful stuff in a yard. You ever stop to think about how stupid we Americans get about this yard business?"

"No, never did."

"Well, think about it. We fertilize and water and pamper the dadgum lawn, and for what? Do we graze it? No. Can we eat it? No. What we can eat in a yard is dandelion greens, but we call the dandelion a weed and spray it with poison."

"Never thought of that."

"We poison what's edible and fertilize what's useless. Now, is that dumb or is that *dumb*?"

"I don't know, Willie, but it's one or the other."

"And that's just the beginning. God put buffalo and grama grass in this country, but do you think anybody will leave God's grass in their yards? No sir. They've got to plow up the natural turf and bring in these unnatural little lickspittle grasses from Kentucky and Florida and Bermuda."

"Yep, sure do."

"And since they don't belong here, they can't stand a hard winter and they can't stand a hot summer, and they have to be pampered and fertilized and mollycoddled."

"Yalp."

"And with all that pampering, the danged stuff *grows*! And then we have to find some fool like me who'll get out and push a lawn mower through it and dump the cuttings behind the tool shed where no animal can eat it and it can't even fertilize the ground it came from."

"Hm. So what you're saying is that mowing the yard is against your religion."

"Yes sir, that's exactly right. It's unnatural, sacrilegious, and sinful. When God was running this show, He took care of the grass and let man do more important things. But we had to stick our big noses into to it, and as usual, we made a mess of it."

Willie sure could pick some strange times to get religion, but I didn't dare tell him that. I just hoped he'd gotten it out of his system so we could enjoy the rest of the day without his gloom and doom.

We made it to the sale barn in time to have our coffee and pie. When the waitress brought the check, we both made a grab for it.

"Let me get that, Willie."

"No, I'll get it. You paid last week."

"Yeah, but you paid the week before."

"Did I? Okay."

He finished his coffee and I had to pay the check. Me and my big mouth.

We visited around for a while and found out some very important information. Joe Bloe had gotten three-tenths of an inch of moisture Sunday night and Pete Endgate had gotten four-tenths. Furthermore, Rollie Bodark had found greenbugs in his wheat. It had been a pretty exciting week.

When the baby calf sale started, we took our usual seats. They ran eight or ten dairy calves through the ring, and by the time the jackpot sale got started, old Willie was asleep.

They sold a crippled cow and a saddle, and then they brought in a billy goat. That was pretty unusual because we don't have many goats in this country. I thought about waking Willie up. I mean, in our part of the world, a guy takes his excitement where he can find it. But I decided to let him sleep.

It kind of surprised me when Willie bobbed his head at the ten dollar bid, and kept bobbing it right up to fifteen-six-bits, and he never did open his eyes that I could see.

"Are you awake?"

He cracked one eye. "What do you think?"

"Do you know that you just bought yourself a billy goat?"

"I just *stole* myself a lawn mower, is what I just did."

I stared at him. "Uh oh. How much do you know about goats?"

"Enough. I know that God built 'em. They're smarter than any machine and they don't have to be pushed. They don't use gas or oil, they don't break down, and they'd just as soon eat a dandelion as anything else."

"True, but . . ."

"I know that you can't buy a lawn mower or three loads of gravel for fifteen bucks. I know that a goat don't buy his fertilizer at the hardware store."

"Yes, but . . ."

"I know that you probably have some silly prejudice against goats, but I also know that you won't bore me with it because you know that I know that you know exactly zero on the subject, so you'll probably keep your uneducated opinions to yourself."

"Oh. Well, I guess that settles it."

"I guess it does." He slapped his knees and pushed himself up. "Let's go. I can't wait to show Iris her new lawn mower."

He paid out and we led Lawn Mower (that's what he named the goat) out to the pickup, hog-tied him with binder twine, and lifted him into the back.

All the way back to the ranch, Willie was smacking his lips and rubbing his hands together and grinning and talking about how "God's lawn mower" was superior to the inventions of man. I hadn't seen him so happy — or so religious — in months. Even the millers didn't bother him when a rough cattle guard brought them out of the heater vents again.

When we got out to the place, he went down to the saddle shed and took a new grass rope off his horn string, tied one end around Lawn Mower's neck and the other around the base of a cherry tree in the front yard.

Sure enough, the goat went right to eating. Willie beamed. "Natural is always best. You can write that down in your little book."

We went into the house and Willie called for Iris. She came into the kitchen and we spent the next forty-five minutes drinking iced tea and listening to Willie's lecture on the follies of modern man. It was pretty good stuff — the iced tea.

G.L. Holmes

Iris was the perfect woman for Willie. There's no telling how many times she'd heard this before, but she just listened and bobbed her head and smiled through it all.

He might have kept going for another half hour, but Iris got up to put her glass in the sink, looked out the window, and said, "I thought you tied up your goat."

Willie almost choked on an ice cube. We rushed out into the yard and discovered that Lawn Mower had eaten Willie's good grass rope and half the cherry tree, had fertilized the sidewalk, was standing on the hood of his car and had pretty well taken care of the paint job.

I wasn't invited to the barbecue, which was all right with me. Among the many things Willie didn't know about goats was that the *-ito* on *cabrito* means "young." Lawn Mower wasn't.

Chapter Four

Willie's Junk Business

In this Panhandle country, we get "dog days" around the middle of August. I don't know who came up with that name, dog days, but it's a good one, very expressive of the way a guy feels about that time of the year.

The weather is hot and the wind quits blowing, and in the afternoon all you can hear is the drone of locusts and the hum of flies and yellow jacket wasps.

It was on one of those dog days that I pulled into Willie Onthenextranch's place. I was desperate for a place to loaf, and knowing Willie as I did, I figured he was in about the same frame of mind.

I checked the house and nobody answered. Iris had gone to town in the car. I checked the shop, one of Willie's hang-outs, but didn't find him there either.

This was beginning to look serious. All at once I was in danger of having to go dig postholes and drive staples. But then, thank heaven, I spotted his pickup down below the corrals.

He'd backed it up to an old bunkhouse, a relic from the days when ranchers could afford employees. It had become a storehouse, and I couldn't imagine what Willie was doing in there.

I stuck my head in the door and saw a miracle in progress. Willie was WORKING! In the heat of the day! Sweat was just pouring off his face.

"Willie, what in the world are you doing in there?"

He squinted at me through the dust, whipped a blue bandanna out of his hip pocket, and mopped his forehead. "After twenty-five years of marital bliss, I'm getting control of our worldly possessions."

I peeked into the back of his pickup. There was an old floor lamp, a couple of cane-back chairs, several stacks of curtains, a roll of used carpet, an upholstered chair, and many other items.

I was impressed. "You mean you're . . ."

"That's right. I'm tired of accumulating junk. Me and Iris set up housekeeping in a two-room shack with a bed, a pot, and a dinner table. That was about right. But then we added the spare bedroom and a family room and this and that, and then we filled it all up with furniture and stuff, and then we started sticking the overflow in this bunkhouse."

"Hm. That sounds familiar."

"And now we've got junk everywhere. It's worse than cancer and grasshoppers. The next to go will be the cakehouse and the feed barn and the shop. Before you know it, we'll be out of the cow business for lack of space."

"What does your lawyer say?"

"Huh?"

"When Iris comes home and finds what you've done, you're liable to need a good lawyer, and maybe a doctor too."

"Ho ho, that's very funny." He leaned his arms on the side of the pickup bed. "Let me tell you something. There comes a time when a man has to decide who owns what. Do we own the junk or does the junk own us?"

"Sounds good, Willie, but there's these fragile little creatures we live with called wives, and a lot of 'em take a dim view of what you're fixing to do."

One corner of his mouth curled in a smirk. "I guess that kind of depends on who's in charge, don't it?"

I nodded. "That's right, Willie, and have you figured out the answer yet?"

"You bet I have." He tapped himself on the chest three times. "Right here."

I smiled. "I'll bet you five bucks you can't pull this off."

"I'll take *ten*."

"You're on."

He grinned and rubbed his hands together. "In that case, you can help me top off this load and we'll head for the dump."

We loaded up some more stuff — an old kitchen cabinet, a baby chair, a trunk, three cases of canning jars, boxes of clothes — and got into the pickup. Willie fired it up and headed for town.

G.L.Holmes

He explained his strategy. "See, instead of pitching all this stuff into that draw behind the barn, I'm gonna haul it to the town junkyard. If I pitched in the draw, old Iris might sneak over there and bring it back, but she's got too much pride to go picking through a public dump."

"That's pretty smart, Willie."

"You got to know these women."

We had just crossed the third cattle guard on the way to town when we passed a car. It was Iris on her way home. At first she waved. Then her mouth dropped open, her eyes widened, and she went off into the ditch looking back at our load.

I expected her to turn the car around and come after us. But she didn't. Willie watched her in the side mirror until she disappeared over a hill.

"She's got her little stubborn streaks but on the whole, she's a pretty good old gal. By the way, I don't take checks for gambling debts. I want my ten bucks in cash."

"You've got a ways to go yet, Willie."

We turned left at the highway and drove towards town, then took a dirt road that led to the town dump. Willie found a clear spot and backed up to it.

We were just about to start pitching the stuff down into the pit when an old guy wearing a greasy felt hat pulled up in a faded green Dodge pickup. He got out and shuffled toward us.

Willie studied him for a minute, then out of the corner of his mouth he whispered, "That's the junk dealer. Watch this."

The old fellow came up and started rubbing the gray whiskers on his cheeks. He had his lips wrapped around a toothpick and he seemed pretty interested in our load.

He and Willie said hello. Then the old feller said, "Why don't you just unload that stuff in my pickup? I might take it off your hands."

Willie got that sparkle in his eyes that comes every time he's about to pull off the deal of the century. "Well, let's talk about that. What'll you give me for the load?"

The old man gave his head a shake. "Oh, I couldn't give you nuthin' for it. It's mostly junk."

"Junk! Listen pardner, these are antiques and treasures and family heirlooms. I couldn't part with 'em for less than a hundred." The old man shook his head. "Unless you gave me fifty." He shook his head. "Twenty-five takes the load." Nope. "Fifteen's my bottom dollar."

The old man rolled the toothpick to the side of his mouth. "Give you five and that's too much."

Willie sighed. "It breaks my heart, but I'll take it."

The old man pulled a long coin purse out of the chest pocket of his bib overalls and pinched out five crumpled dollar bills. We moved the junk into his pickup and he drove off to town.

Willie was almost beside himself. He giggled and rubbed his hands and then snapped his fingers and held his palm out to me. "Ten bucks please. It's a real business doing pleasure with you." I paid off.

We'd gotten back in the pickup when we noticed a plume of dust on the horizon. It was coming down the road at a high rate of speed. Willie grumbled something about crazy drivers and was about to pull away from the junkyard when Iris slid to a stop.

She didn't look real happy, and she crooked her finger at someone in our pickup. Willie swallowed hard and chewed at his lip.

"What do you reckon she's doing out on this lonely road?" I asked.

He shot me a glare. "Don't you worry about it." He got out, shoved his hands into his pockets, and walked over to the car.

Their discussion didn't last long. Willie climbed back into the pickup and headed for town. He didn't say a word and I had a feeling that this was a real good time for me to honor the silence.

We pulled up to the junk shop just as the old man was lifting the first chair out of his pickup. Willie got out and kicked a couple of rocks.

"I got to have my junk back. I'll refund your money."

The old man frowned and shook his head. "What junk you talking about?"

"My stuff, right there in your pickup."

"Oh. You mean these antiques? No, I already got some buyers in mind."

Willie tapped his toe and studied the ground. "I'll give you ten."

"Naw, I've got labor and time and gas tied up in this load . . ."

"Fifteen."

" . . . and you know, I've got three customers here in town who've been pestering me for months to find 'em antiques just like these . . ."

"Twenty."

" . . . and this antique market has really gone crazy . . ."

"Twenty-five and not one penny more!"

The old fellow hooked his thumbs in his overalls and looked up at the sky. "I could haul this stuff to Amarillo and make a small fortune on it." He studied Willie's face, which was turning redder by the second. "Tell you what, though, I'll sacrifice it for fifty bucks."

"You're a crook, is what you are."

"Fifty-five."

Willie whipped out his checkbook and wrote a check. "There! I hope you break out in hives."

The old man slid a pair of dime store glasses on his nose and looked at the check. "I believe you forgot to sign it," he smiled, handing it back. Willie slashed his name across the bottom line. "Sure thank you, and yall boys come back again."

He sat down in a lawn chair and watched us transfer the load back into Willie's rig. On the way out to the ranch, Willie got tuned up and delivered one of his better sermons.

"You know what's wrong with America today? We got vultures on every corner. Nobody gives a hoot any more for the old-time values or help your neighbor."

"Boy, that's the truth."

"Everybody's out for the big fast buck."

"That's right." We flew over the last cattle guard and pulled up in front of the bunk house. "Which reminds me. You've got ten big fast bucks of mine."

He turned to me with a smoldering glare. He dug my ten dollar bill out of his wallet and slapped it into my palm. "You're no better than the rest of them."

"I know it, Willie. Sometimes I can hardly stand myself. Now, you've given my ten back and you owe me ten more for losing the bet."

He jerked another ten out and threw it at me. "There, take it! How about some blood? How about some skin or my wooden leg or my granddaughter's doll baby?"

"No, this'll hold me for a couple of days." I got out of the pickup. "Say, Willie, did you ever figure out whether you own this junk or it owns you?" At that point, Willie's language got too naughty to repeat.

Chapter Five

Willie's Plumbing

It started off as a simple plumbing problem. Iris, our neighbor's wife, had found a leak under the kitchen sink. Nothing terribly serious, just a slow drip, something a well-equipped plumber could have fixed in 15 or 20 minutes.

What made it serious was that she had found it a month before and had been dropping hints to Willie on a regular basis, suggesting that he might want to do something about it.

Willie had always come up with a good reason for putting it off. "Tell you what, I'll fix your sink if you'll fix my windmills." And, "Listen, Iris, I've got seven heavy heifers down there in the lot. Let me get 'em calved out and we'll see where we are." And, "I'll get right on it, hon, just as soon as I get caught up."

That went on for a month. Iris stopped hinting. Maybe Willie thought the leak had fixed itself. Then one day after lunch, he heard his wife in the next room, talking on the phone. Curious, he listened and soon pieced together the awful truth: she had called a plumber!

By the time she came back into the kitchen, old Willie had worked himself into a fit of righteous anger.

"What do you mean, calling a dad-danged plumber!"

"Well," she said, "when people have plumbing problems, they call a plumber."

"Maybe town folks do, but we ain't town folks. We live on a ranch."

"Yes, I know that, dear."

"Maybe you also knew that plumbers charge $25 an hour and they start the meter running when they leave the shop and then naturally they have to stop at the Dairy Queen and get a soda pop, and besides all that, they have to bring an assistant to hold their wrench for them. Before they get done, that leak's worth two hundred dollars."

"That's very expensive, isn't it?"

"It's more than expensive, Iris. It's criminal!"

She shook her head. "It's too bad there's not another way of getting my plumbing problem fixed."

"What you've got ain't a plumbing problem, it's a simple leak. Anybody can fix a simple leak."

"Yes, but it's been a month now and I know how busy you've been and I think it's time . . ."

"I'm unbusy, right now." He flew out of his chair and slammed his old hat down on his head. "I'm going for my wrenches, and you call that plumber and tell him that this outfit can take care of itself, and before we'll need a plumber, we'll need an undertaker!"

Willie stormed out of the house. Iris went on watering her hanging plants. She didn't call the plumber back because she hadn't called him in the first place. After years of dealing with Willie, she had learned how to get results.

I pulled in just as he came flying out of his shop, swinging his hat at a bunch of angry wasps. I guess he'd managed to get them stirred up.

I walked toward him, enjoying the nice warm sun. "Looks like your yellowjackets wintered well."

He gave me the evil eye and pointed to a welt on his cheek. "I got stung, so if you came down here to make jokes, maybe you'd better just keep driving."

I tried to bite back a smile. "Sorry to hear that, Willie."

"No you ain't, but then you probably didn't realize that last year, more people died of bug bites than snake bites, so it's no laughing matter."

I managed to steer my laugh into a cough. "It sure isn't. In fact, it's very . . ." I turned my head and, uh, coughed again. ". . . very serious."

"You better believe it." He rubbed the welt, which had begun to swell and was giving his left eye an Oriental slant. "Fool wasps. I hate 'em."

He went back into the shop and I followed. "What are you up to this beautiful spring afternoon?"

He went to the work bench which was piled with tools, windmill checks and leathers, pieces of pipe, copper tubing, jet rod wrenches, stock trailer bearings, and other items too numerous to mention. He began plundering through the mess, jerking out a wrench here and a screwdriver there.

"I'm trying to keep this ranch from sliding into bankruptcy." He told me about the plumber. By that time he had collected his wrenches and we started back to the house. "They can charge the rest of the world that 25 bucks an hour, plus mileage, plus coffee breaks, plus hazard pay, but on this outfit, we do our own plumbing."

I could hardly wait. I had planned to spend the afternoon patching up a mile of fence in the west pasture, but I had a feeling I wouldn't want to miss this.

"Can I help you?"

"No help needed, thanks. Just stay out of the way and don't ask dumb questions."

"All right."

Willie breezed into the house, pitched his greasy hat on the dinner table, ordered Iris out of the room, opened the cabinet doors under the sink, studied the copper water lines for a moment, announced that he had found the source of the leak, and put his wrench on the joint where the tubing tied into the pipe.

I noticed there wasn't a shut-off valve below the tubing. "Willie, can I ask you one question?"

"No. I'm a busy man. If you want to learn about plumbing, go to the library and check out . . ."

On about the fourth turn of the wrench, he struck water. It sprayed him in the face. He got it stopped, scrambled out, wiped his face, and gave me a withering glare. Then he went down to the storage tank and shut off the main valve to the house.

"How come you didn't put a shut-off valve on those sink lines?"

He rolled his eyes. "Because they cost $2.50 apiece. Because they're unnecessary. Because I watch my expenses. Any more silly questions?"

Just as he entered the house, Iris came in. "Willie, I think the toilet's broken. It won't flush."

He sighed. "No, the toilet ain't broke, I just shut off the water to the house and I'll have everything running again in five minutes if people will just leave me alone."

She shrugged and left the room. Willie grumbled and crawled back under the sink. Three minutes later, he emerged with a stalk of copper tubing. He seemed in a better mood now. He pointed to one end.

"There's the problem. All we have to do is cut it, flare it, and stick it back on. And for that little piece of work, I've saved this ranch two hundred bucks. That's pretty good wages for a cowboy, ain't it?"

I didn't say anything. Willie got his cutting tool, cut off the bad end, and did a beautiful job of flaring the new end so that it would fit nice and snug inside the brass coupling, except that the brass coupling was sitting on the edge of the sink. He'd forgotten to slip it back on the tubing.

When he saw what he'd done, he raised his eyes to me. I was smiling. "It could happen to anyone," I said.

He said nothing, but whacked off the flared end, put the coupling back on the tubing, and did another flare job. As he was crawling back under the sink, I said, "I hope it still fits."

"It'll fit, don't you worry."

But it didn't. If you've ever worked with copper tubing, you know that "pretty close" isn't close enough. Willie came up a half-inch short, even though he did his best to pull the sink down and the floor up.

He wasn't happy when he came out from under the sink. I followed him down to the shop and watched him go through his collection of copper tubing which he had salvaged from heaven-knows-where and had kept for who-knows-how-long. He had every size of tubing except three-eights, which happened to be what he needed.

It took him an hour to make this discovery. He just kept looking — in the shop, in the garage, in the medicine shed, in the cake house. Finally the truth soaked in.

"Well," I said, "I reckon you'll have to make a trip into town."

That was the wrong thing to say. It got him stirred up again.

"You think so? Well, let me tell you something, Bub. Our ancestors settled this country without running to the danged lumber yard every minute, and that same old pioneer spirit is still alive on this outfit. On this ranch, we make do."

"Oh. Okay."

"We use our brains, see? We figger out how to take what we've got and make it work. And no, we don't run into town to buy eighteen inches of copper tubing — ever."

I sat down on a feed bucket and spent a pleasant hour and a half watching Willie figure out how to go from three-eights copper to half-inch pipe to five-eighths copper back to three-eighths copper.

He cut and he spliced and he flared and he smeared pipe dope and he cussed. And then he gloated over his new invention. It looked like the insides of a submarine or an atomic reactor. He had managed to turn a dollar's worth of copper tubing into $25 worth of unions, elbows, and brass fittings.

G.L. Holmes

"That's nice, Willie, but I think you'd have to admit that in the time it took you to rig that thing up, you could have gone to town and bought what you needed."

I felt the heat of his scowl. "You fit right into this modern consumer society, where everybody runs to the danged store 32 times a day and nobody knows how to patch up, make do, and get along. Well, this cowboy," he tapped himself on the chest, "has seen hard times and knows how to live off the land."

I nodded. He still hadn't got it all stuck back together.

We walked back to the house. I noticed that the sun was getting low in the west. "Well, one thing about it, Willie. Even if you wanted to go to town now, it's too late. The stores are already closed."

"Fine. If they wait for my business, they'll stay closed."

Iris met us at the door. "Willie, I need some water to get supper started."

"Never fear, madame. Willie the Wizard has just notched up another victory. We'll have water in ten minutes."

He crawled back under the sink and I listened to the clanking of his wrenches. Ten minutes passed. Then . . . silence.

"You want me to turn on the main valve?" I asked.

I could see his eyes in the darkness — well, one of them. The other was almost swollen shut. "No, I don't want you to turn on the valve. I want you to get in your pickup and go home."

"How come?"

He stood up and dusted off his pants. "Because it's time for you to go home and your wife's probably worrying about you."

He led me outside. "Oh, I don't think so, Willie."

"Yes, she is. I'm sure she is." He opened the door of my pickup. "Bye. Come back when you can't stay so long."

"Well, if you're sure I can't help you any more . . ."

"I'm sure. Bye."

I went home. A couple of days later, I learned that in hooking up the sink line, he'd twisted off a water pipe. He and Iris made a dry camp that night and brushed their teeth down at the stock tank.

The next morning, Iris sent him out into the pasture and called the plumber. By noon, they had water again — and the plumber's bill only came to $197.50.

Which just goes to prove something about cowboy-plumbers. If necessity is the mother of invention, it's also the grandmother of comedy.

Chapter Six

Willie's Insurance

It must have been last Thursday. No, it was Wednesday. No, it was Monday.

Oh well, I guess it doesn't matter much. Around here, one day is pretty much like another. Good thing we have calendars. A guy sure ought to know that today ain't last week.

I was roosting up on top of a windmill, tightening down the fan bolts, when I saw a pickup coming across the pasture. It was Willie Onthenextranch, and he was driving fast.

Uh, oh, I thought, he's ready to dig out that water line. I'd told him I'd help. I gathered up my tools and started down the ladder to hear the bad news.

Willie slid to a stop and jumped out. "Hey, did you hear Paul Harvey today?"

"Some people have to work for a living. No."

G.L. Holmes

By this time, Willie had that crazy look in his eyes that he gets every time he thinks he's figgered a way to make money on cattle.

"This may be it! This just might turn things around."

I sat down on the tailgate. "Okay, I'm ready to hear it."

He was rubbing his hands together. "Paul Harvey says there's a woman doctor in New York, an expert, who thinks all young couples ought to take out divorce insurance before they get married. That way, when they decide to split the blanket, the insurance will pay the cost of the divorce."

I stared at him. "You came all the way out here to tell me *that*?"

"Just a minute, I'm coming to the important part." He hitched up his pants. I don't know why, but Willie always does that when he comes to the important parts of things. "All right, lookie here. Two people swear before God and the law that they'll stay hitched, till death do impart. That's a contract, ain't it?"

"It used to be. Nowadays . . ."

"Now, if a guy can take out insurance to break that contract, why couldn't he get insurance on other things?"

"Willie . . ."

"Hush, I ain't through. Now, you take feed. It's awful high this year. Why couldn't a man contract about a hundred ton of cottonseed cake, feed it up, and then tell the feed store that he wanted out of the deal?"

"Well, for one thing . . ."

"Then the insurance would pay off, and that would be the end of it."

"That's crooked."

His chin came up. "It ain't crooked. It's insurance. The thing is, if everybody had contract-breaking insurance, we wouldn't have any crooks. The courts wouldn't even need to get involved. The insurance would take care of everything, see?"

"And what's to keep the insurance companies from going broke?"

"Simple." He poked me in the chest. "The government will insure the insurance companies. Haven't you ever heard of the FDIC? Same sort of deal."

"Then the government will go broke."

Willie laughed. "Nope. Get this." He glanced over both shoulders and moved closer. "The government will buy insurance from the Russians. The more contracts we break over here, the more money the Russkies will have to pay out. That way, breaking contracts won't be against the law, it'll be patriotic!"

"Willie . . ."

"The way I figger it, in five good years we'll have them Russkies stone broke. No more balance of payments problems. No more inflation. And all we have to do is act natural — lie, cheat, and swindle."

I put up my tools. "That's great, Willie. You've really come up with a winner this time."

"It beats working for a living."

"I guess so."

His mood darkened. "And speaking of four-letter words, me and you have some *work* to do."

"Oh?"

"That's right. You said you'd help me dig up that water line."

"I said that?"

"Yes you did, you certainly did."

"You mean I promised? Gave you my word? We had a verbal contract?"

His eyes narrowed. "What are you . . ."

"It's getting close to my nap time, Willie. I think I'll back out of the deal."

"Now, wait a minute."

"And if you don't like it, you can call my insurance man — Russian feller named Ivan Skavinski Skavar. Have fun with your water line."

I hopped into my pickup and drove off.

Served him right, the old sneak.

Chapter Seven

Our Little Animal Friends

Every writer finds his own way of learning what he needs to know about life and human nature. I spent eight years working as a cowboy in the Texas and Oklahoma Panhandles.

That's a long time, and it was a hard way to get an education. Surely medical science will invent a pill that will cure ignorance in a month or two. But maybe not. We have stamped out smallpox and leprosy but ignorance seems to resist our best efforts.

Now that I have retired from active service as a ranch hand, I have the opportunity to look back on my experiences and think about what I learned. One of the things that has occurred to me recently is that I benefited from living and working around animals.

As odd as it may sound, there are certain insights to be gained in observing the behavior of cattle and horses.

One of the first things you learn about cattle is that they aren't very bright. Some people would even say they're stupid. I have said that more times than I can remember.

Cattle have been known to die of thirst in pastures where water was available. Cattle will trample and befoul their own feed and then walk away hungry. They have been known to swallow bones, barbed wire, fencing pliers, and bits of metal, leading to a medical condition known as "hardware stomach."

Cattle are notorious for resisting the efforts of cowboys to save them from disease, wounds, parasites, and calving problems. There are times when it appears that cattle are just not smart enough to survive in this world.

Yet just about the time you're on the point of believing that cattle are the stupidest, most feather-headed, brainless creatures God ever invented, it occurs to you that no cow has ever built a hydrogen bomb.

There are also valuable lessons to be learned from observing horses. Horses have gotten better press than cattle and are usually perceived as noble animals. In this they may have been helped more by their good looks than by their actions.

Anyone who is thinking of becoming a misanthrope should spend some time around horses. One of the follies of my youth was thinking that human beings have a patent on greed and pettiness. We don't. We share it with horses.

Human history is recreated by horses every morning at feeding time. Equine nobility evaporates when you pour some feed into a trough. The fact that they're all fat, sleek, and well-fed doesn't matter. The fact that some of them may be papered and listed on the tax rolls at incredible prices doesn't matter.

When the first kernel of corn or oats hits the trough, they pin back their ears, curl their lips, make dives at each other, bite, butt, kick, gouge, snarl, and squeal over the grub.

When possible, they will avoid a fair fight, choosing instead to intimidate the young, the small, the newly arrived, the aged, and the handicapped. Given the slightest opportunity, a horse will eat everything in sight and literally eat itself to death. (By contrast, the lowly mule will eat its fill and walk away, unfoundered).

The only thing that saves a horse from dying of his own greed is the greed of his companions.

In his book *The Fiddleback: Lore of the Line Camp*, Owen Ulph made the observation that if horses could talk, they would lie. I'd guess that if horses could talk, they'd talk about nothing but eating, and their conversation would be so boring that no one could stand to listen to them.

Another trait of horses that isn't well known to the general public is that they spend a great deal of time trying to figure out how to avoid work. Teen-age boys may be worse about this than horses, but not by much.

I used to ride a half-Arabian named Reno. Under saddle and out in the pasture, he was a work of art — a slashing, dashing, daring brute with a heart as big as a watermelon. He had enough speed to scare you to death, enough quickness to throw you out of the saddle, enough endurance to make you wish he would take it easy once in a while.

By any standard, he was a great work horse — but getting the son of a gun caught and bridled so that he could show his stuff was a major ordeal.

If he knew you were going to put him to work, he would walk away, slink away, run away, buck away, skip away, stick his head into a corner, dash around the corral, stamp his feet, snort, and hold his head so high in the air that you needed a six-foot stepladder to install the bit.

He knew and employed every subterfuge short of calling in sick, and he missed that one only because he didn't own a telephone. Left to his own devices, he would have been a complete bum.

Stalking him around the corral in the first dim light of day, I used to ask him, "Reno, what would you do if I didn't make you work for a living? The only time you distinguish yourself is when you're out in the pasture. Around the barn, you're nothing but an alimentary tract with a tail on the end of it. Do you really think you'd be happier if all you did was eat and swat flies?"

G.L. Holmes

I think his answer would have been yes — yes without hesitation, yes without a moment's thought, yes without a shred of remorse. His greatest ambition was to have no ambition. His highest aspiration was to reach a state of biology where the electrons in his body moved just enough to avoid decomposition.

There has always been a bond between man and horse. It could be that of all the animals in the world, we are the only two species that believe that doing nothing is something worth doing.

Reno and I worked together for more than four years. In my old age I'll remember him as the horse of horses, the one I'd like to ride through the clouds in the afterlife. He'll always be in my personal hall of fame.

Of course I won't forget how he made it to my hall of fame — at gunpoint, under protest and only after all else had failed. If it hadn't been for me, Reno would have been crowbait.

In some odd way, I find the parallels between animal and human behavior encouraging. How can you tumble into misanthropy when you realize that the anthropes that you miss are simply part of a larger natural system?

I mean, isn't it good news that we're not the only creatures on this earth who eat too much and bicker over nothing? That horses love mediocrity and sloth just as much as we? That cattle were behaving stupidly centuries before we tried it?

It might be argued that we humans have been more successful at building institutions upon our bad habits, but it's good to know that we didn't invent them.

Chapter Eight

Ace Reid's Cabin In The Woods

One evening in September 1984, while I was down at the Draggin' S Ranch near Kerrville, Texas, working on the biography of western artist Ace Reid, Ace's wife Madge pulled several dusty boxes out of a hall closet.

They contained sketches that Ace had done as a young man, before he gained his national reputation as the creator of the *Cowpokes* cartoon series. They were very good, and quite different from the kind of work he did in later years.

I made up my mind then that some day I would return to the Draggin' S Ranch and put those drawings together into an Ace Reid Sketchbook and bring it out through Maverick Books.

That opportunity came the following summer. On July 4, Kris and I packed the van with clothes, writing equipment, four kids, and a dog, and made the eleven-hour drive from Perryton to Kerrville. We arrived around midnight and moved into a hunters' cabin, off in the woods about a quarter mile from the Reid house.

Through the month of July, the cabin was home to me, Kris, Scot, Ashley, little Mark, and Scot's friend from Branson, Missouri, Mark Sherman. We ate and slept in the cabin's one big room, which had a big rock fireplace at one end and a kitchen on the other. In between were a dining bar, a rough table and chairs, four beds, and after the first day, a lot of dirty socks and tennis shoes.

On the walls hung deer antlers, coon pelts, deer hides, the head of a javalina, and various mementos from Ace's career.

Camping in the woods required some adjustments in our life style. The first day, when Ashley stepped into the bathtub, she discovered that the electric water heater had a short in it, and that any time it was plugged in, you could expect a jolt of electricity.

When I complained to Ace about this, he said, "That's sure too bad. Maybe you'd better fix it before one of them kids gets electrocuted."

Ace was about as mechanically inclined as his dog, and I got no help out of either one of them. I solved the problem by instructing the family to unplug the water heater before anyone got into the tub. It worked, but I noticed that little Ashley had an allergy to bathtubs for the rest of the summer.

Our water came straight out of the creek nearby — out of our favorite swimming hole, actually — and we never knew what kinds of vitamins and minerals we were getting along with our drinking water. After a rain, when the creek came up, a tub of bath water was likely to be muddy even before the kids climbed in.

We got a first-rate education in a type of wildlife that we didn't have back home in the Panhandle — ticks and chiggers. After two weeks of tramping through the woods, the boys and I resembled victims of smallpox. The chiggers practically ate our legs off.

The ticks weren't as bad as the chiggers. At least you could see the ticks or feel them crawling up your leg. Checking each other for ticks became part of our evening's entertainment. Just about any evening, as the sun slipped behind the big hill to the west, we would be gathered in our (unairconditioned) cabin. Kris would hold two-year old Mark down on the bed with a leg-lock while Ashley checked his ears and armpits for ticks.

On the average day, while I was up at the studio interviewing Ace or going through a pile of sketches, Mark Sherman and Scot would be off in the woods, chasing armadillos or working on their log cabin. Kris, Ashley, and little Mark might be paddling around on inner tubes in our swimming hole, which was just a short walk from the cabin.

The boys kept us well supplied with pets, and there were times when our place resembled a branch of the San Antonio Zoo. We provided a home for three armadillos, three snakes, two turtles, an orphan fawn, half a dozen frogs, and an uncounted number of tadpoles and crawdads.

This was in addition to our dog Scamper and Ace's cur, Ugly the Killer Dog.

There were several days we won't forget, such as the day the photographer from *Texas Highways* magazine was out shooting pictures for an article on Ace. Little Mark, who was as bold and curious as a raccoon, slipped out of the living room. By the time Kris realized that he had disappeared, he was sitting in the middle of Ace's bed, eating prescription medicine.

We didn't know which of Ace's pills he might have eaten: high blood pressure pills, pills for diabetes, or plain old aspirin. But we couldn't take any chances. In the middle of the the picture-taking session, we scooped him up and made the twenty-minute drive into town.

It was a bad road — rough and rocky with blind curves and low-water crossings. Ace and Madge had once met each other on that road, in a head-on collision, and had totaled both family cars. Fortunately, we didn't have that problem.

In the emergency room, we paced the floor while the doctor pumped Marky's stomach. It turned out that he had swallowed only a small amount of medicine and he was all right. The trip to town only cost us a hundred bucks.

But for the next several weeks Ace was on a tear. He complained that his medicine bill had doubled during our stay, and that his cat food bill was three times the usual rate — this because of Mark's habit of eating with Ace's cats.

It was embarrassing. The boy would eat anything that didn't try to eat him first. Of course, Ace loved it, and every time he told about Marky's eating habits, the story got bigger and wilder. By the end of the summer, Ace was telling his friends that Mark had chewed down two of his pecan trees.

Another memorable day came when we took Ace to the dentist to have a jaw tooth pulled. When he emerged, he presented Ashley with a necklace made of the freshly extracted tooth, strung on a piece of dental floss.

Not only that, but he had his dentist write up a certificate of authenticity, stating that the "stone" in the necklace was a genuine Ace Reid tooth, one of a limited edition of thirty-two.

While this was going on, Ashley looked up at Uncle Ace with wide blue eyes and a puzzled smile. She had herself a real collector's piece there, but she didn't know quite what to think about it.

She isn't the first to wonder what to make of Ace Reid, and she probably won't be the last either.

After a five-week stay in the cabin, we made our way back to the Panhandle to get the children ready for school. We were still scratching our chiggers and tick bites, but we had survived our summer in the woods.

But back home, we began to notice that everyone's hair had an oily, matted look, even after shampooing. Kris became suspicious and gave Ashley's scalp a close examination. To her horror, she found little vermin crawling around on her daughter's head.

We had lice, every one of us.

Kris swallowed her pride and went down to the Corner Drug and asked Chris Vines what she should do about it. Between chuckles, Mr. Vines sold her a bottle of evil-smelling gunk and a couple of nit picks, and told her to shampoo the whole family with the sheep dip, wash the bed linens, and use the nit picks several times a day to get rid of the louse eggs.

It took us weeks to get rid of the cursed lice, and Ashley suffered the humiliation of being sent home by the school nurse who spotted a few nits in her hair. That ruined her chances of being voted Sweetheart of Room 1-B.

I reported all this to Ace. I thought he might be concerned — if not about the social stigma that had attached itself to the Erickson name, then at least about the presence of lice in his cabin. After all, he planned to lease the cabin out to deer hunters in the fall.

But Ace was a humorist. For twenty-five years he had made his living by finding the humor in what other mortals regarded as disaster.

He laughed so hard, he dropped the telephone. When he came back on the line, he said, "By gollies, John, I just might get a cartoon out of that story!"

As of this writing, three years later, we have not returned to Ace's cabin in the woods.

Chapter Nine

The Jones Ghost House

It has always been hard to distinguish prophets from scoundrels, since they often wear the same clothes.

As I write this in March of 1987, the newspapers are buzzing with stories about a television evangelist named Jim Bakker who, it appears, wasn't the man his followers thought he was when they sent him $130 million dollars last year.

The preacher-turned-rascal is a recurring story in American history, and a few years ago I ran across a version of it in my own little part of the world, the Texas Panhandle. I first heard about the Jones Ghost House in 1971 when I was gathering material for *Through Time and the Valley*. A lady in Canadian, Texas, happened to mention it when we were talking about another matter.

She said that when she was a child, the whole northern Panhandle was in an uproar about a haunted house on Wolf Creek. But that's all she could remember about it.

From then on, when I interviewed an old-timer about the history of the Canadian River, which was my subject in that first book, I asked if he knew anything about the haunted house on Wolf Creek. Most could remember hearing about it but none could give me any details.

For months I tried to chase the story down, with no luck. Then one day in January 1972 I walked into a store on Perryton's Main Street and said to the owner, "I've spent months trying to find someone who could tell me about the Jones Ghost House. I've been told that you might know something about it."

The old man grinned and pointed to a couple of chairs in front of a big open-front gas stove. Yes, he knew the story. We sat down and he spent the next hour telling it.

In 1909 the Jones family owned a small ranch on Wolf Creek, south of Perryton. There were two houses on the ranch, one on each side of the creek. The Joneses lived in the newer house on the south side, while the older one, a two-story affair on the north bank, was vacant.

Isaac Jones was a respected rancher in the area. When the county had first been settled in the late 1880s, he had served as county commissioner. He had a solid reputation.

One day he received a letter from a cousin of his, Jasper Jones, who was a fire-and-brimstone preacher in Missouri. Jasper had lost his wife and lived alone with his daughter, Maude. Times were hard in Missouri, he said, and he wanted to move to the Panhandle and live in the empty house on the ranch.

If Isaac would let him stay in the old house, rent-free, he would help with the ranch work during the week and do some preaching on Sundays.

Isaac felt sorry for his cousin, and although he didn't particularly admire him, he told him to come on out and they'd give it a try.

So Jasper and Maudie moved into the old house on the north side of the creek. As he had promised, he helped with the ranch work during the week and preached in a little one-room schoolhouse on Sundays. He was quite a showman in the pulpit, and it was said that nobody slept through his sermons.

All went well for six months or so, but then problems developed between the cousins. Jasper had a devious side to his nature and he tried to exploit every situation to his own advantage. He was the kind of relative who made himself right at home and tended to forget that he was a guest.

Isaac took it as long as he could, and then he came down hard on Jasper and told him to straighten out. Jasper sulled up and said no more. But he began thinking of a way to ruin Cousin Isaac.

It happened that Isaac and his family had been planning to make a trip to Indiana to visit family, and they would be gone for a month or so. Jasper assured his cousin that he would take care of the ranch, and so Isaac left with a good feeling, little suspecting that Jasper was nursing a grudge against him.

Jasper knew that his cousin had once employed a cowboy named Larue. This fellow had worked on the ranch for a while and then had left without a trace. This wasn't unusual for the times. Cowboys moved around in those days and often left without saying goodbye or leaving a forwarding address.

But Jasper decided to make something out of Larue's disappearance. He began whispering around that his cousin had *murdered* him!

Jasper claimed that Larue had saved up several hundred dollars and kept it tied in a white silk handkerchief. One night Isaac sneaked up the stairs and killed him in his bed. According to Jasper, Cousin Isaac struck him once with an axe, then delivered three more strokes to make sure he was dead, just as the clock downstairs chimed the hour — ten o'clock.

Then, according to Jasper's tale, Isaac dragged the body down to the creek, weighed it down with rocks, and threw it into a deep pool. He buried the money under some rocks nearby.

You'd think that the people of Ochiltree County would have dismissed that story as wild gossip. After all, they had lived around Isaac Jones for years and had even elected him to a county office. Jasper, on the other hand, was an outsider.

But Jasper was a clever man. He knew how to feed a small fire and make a blaze out of it. And it helped that the "murderer" had left the country.

"Why did Cousin Isaac leave all of a sudden?" Jasper would say. "I'm sure I don't know. How could he afford to make such a trip? Well, I just couldn't answer that."

The story went through the neighborhood like a prairie fire, and before long people were coming around and asking Jasper if it were true.

"I'm afraid it is," Jasper told them. "I know, because Larue's ghost is still in that old house. If you want the proof, just come around tonight at 9:30. That's when Larue's ghost comes out."

So that night a crowd of people came to the house. They sat in the living room and listened as Jasper told them that he had no fear of ghosts because he was a preacher. A ghost wouldn't harm a man of God.

Then, with all the theatrical skill he had used in his Sunday sermons, he recreated the scene of the crime. "My cousin hit him in the head with the axe," he said in a low voice, "and then he hit him *three more times*!"

All at once they all heard a thump upstairs. It was followed by three more thumps.

"There's Larue's ghost now!" Jasper cried. "He's telling you how many times he was hit with the axe!"

And just then the clock chimed out the hour: ten o'clock. At that point Jasper asked his daughter to stand up. He explained that little Maudie, age 10, was a psychic medium and that Larue's ghost could speak through her. The girl closed her eyes and stood perfectly still for a minute or two. No one spoke.

Then she began walking up the stairs. Jasper picked up a kerosene lamp and motioned for the others to follow.

Up the stairs she went. She walked into one of the bedrooms and stopped. Jasper held the lamp high and pointed to a dark red stain on the floor.

"Look there! A blood stain! Larue was murdered in this very room, and Maudie has brought us to the spot."

Well, that *did* make a story. Before long, people all over the northern Panhandle were buzzing about the murder and the ghost house. Some people even said that Isaac Jones should be lynched if he ever returned.

One man who didn't believe the story was Sid Talley, the sheriff of Ochiltree County. Talley was new on the job, having been elected to the office the year before after a blizzard had forced him out of the ranching business.

He was a small, wiry man who never carried a gun. He always figured that if a lawman used his head, he wouldn't need to use a gun.

He didn't believe Jasper's story about the murder, and he was alarmed by the intense feelings the preacher was whipping up. He decided to go to the haunted house and look around.

He picked a time when Jasper wasn't around, went into the old house on the north side of the creek, and set the clock back one hour.

That night Jasper had a group over to hear the story. At the appropriate time, the clock struck *nine* and the ghost appeared anyway. Sheriff Talley was in the group that night, and he counted the chimes of the clock.

Something was fishy here. Either the ghost couldn't count very well or Jasper was making it all up. He suspected the latter, but he kept his thoughts to himself.

Not long after this incident, Jasper put out the word that Larue's ghost was going to lead him to the spot where the money had been buried. Cousin Isaac had probably dug it up long ago, but maybe they could find a trace of it.

A crowd of twenty people gathered at the ghost house that night, including Sheriff Talley. When the clock struck ten (Jasper had reset it), Maudie went into a trance and walked out of the house.

G.L. Holmes

Carrying a lantern and a shovel, Jasper followed, and the crowd came along behind him. Maudie walked down the steps and out into the night. When she came to a little knoll down near the creek, she stopped.

Jasper rushed up with his shovel and began to dig away the rocks. As the hole deepened, he threw down the shovel and began digging with his hands.

Then he stopped digging. He reached into the hole and pulled out a white silk handkerchief. Tied in one end was a rusted nickel. The crowd gasped, as Jasper passed the coin around. Sheriff Talley examined it and passed it on.

His sharp eye had noticed an interesting detail. Larue was supposed to have been murdered in 1905. The date on the coin was 1906.

Now he was sure the murder story was a hoax, but since Jasper hadn't actually broken any laws, he couldn't arrest him. About all he could do was try to cool the tempers of the local citizens, warn Isaac Jones when he returned home, and see that he wasn't lynched before the matter was cleared up.

When Isaac started back to Texas, his train laid over a few hours in Wichita, Kansas. He got a bite to eat and stretched his legs. While he was eating, he heard people at the next table talking about a ghastly murder that had occurred somewhere down in Texas. They said something about a haunted house, and then they named the murderer: *Isaac Jones*.

He left his meal uneaten and hurried back to the train. When he reached his destination, the little town of Glazier, Texas, he heard more talk about the murder. The town buzzed with the story. He slipped through town, hiding his face and telling no one his name, hired a wagon and started home.

He went straight to the town of Ochiltree, until 1919 the county seat of Ochiltree County, and looked up his friend Sheriff Talley. He asked Sid what on earth was going on, and the sheriff told him the whole story. They agreed that it was time for Cousin Jasper to leave the country.

Isaac was furious. He drove out to the ranch, loaded up a pistol, and hunted up his cousin. "Jasper," he said, "there isn't a ghost around this place right now, but if you're still here tomorrow, there will be."

Looking into the bore of Isaac's pistol, Jasper agreed that it might be a good time to return to Missouri. He threw Maudie and their belongings into a wagon and left the country.

When Jasper left, the hoax was exposed, tempers cooled, and life returned to normal. Sheriff Talley had located Larue, the "murdered" cowboy, somewhere in the southern Panhandle and had received a letter from him, saying that he would come to Ochiltree and appear before a grand jury, if that became necessary.

How had Jasper managed to pull off such a hoax? Well, he was a spellbinding preacher who knew how to play on peoples' emotions. But he had other talents as well. During his career as a revivalist, he had learned ventriloquism and hypnotism. To simulate the thumps in the upstairs bedroom, he had thrown his voice, and little Maudie had performed her role under hypnosis.

The dark stain on the floor? Chicken blood.

And finally, Jasper seemed to understand a principle of human nature that has been exploited by charlatans and scoundrels throughout the ages: Small lies are easy to dismiss, but the bigger the lie, the more plausible it becomes.

That's a good thing to remember because, while Jasper Jones departed this earth many years ago, his kind is born anew in every generation.

Chapter 10

Roping Wild Horses In The Library of Congress

It isn't every Texas cowboy who gets a chance to rope a wild horse in the nation's capitol, but I did. In January of 1983 I got a call from the Library of Congress. The caller explained that the Library was putting together a big exhibit on the American cowboy which would open in March.

The opening in Washington was going to be a big affair, and the Library planned to fly in several working cowboys to speak at a symposium. They had also invited five or six western scholars to give papers on the same program.

Since I had spent eight years ahorseback and had written a few books on the subject, they wondered if I could come.

Well, naturally I was honored, and since the taxpayers would be picking up all the bills, I didn't see how I could lose. I accepted the invitation, and in March I climbed on a plane in Amarillo and flew to Washington. In my suitcase I carried my best pasture rope.

I caught a taxi from the airport and checked into a very dignified hotel not far from the Library of Congress — Ebbitt House, I think it was called. It was fancy enough so that the word "hotel" didn't appear in the name.

They had three varieties of soap beside the sink, one for your hands, one for your face, and I don't know what the other one was for. Your feet, maybe. I used 'em all and had a wonderful time in the bathtub. Never been so clean.

Another thing they had in the bathroom was one of those French drinking fountains beside the toilet. I tried it out and I can tell you that drinking out of one of those things ain't easy.

I had to get down on my hands and knees, and then when I turned the handle, the thing shot out a stream of water that just about knocked my glasses off. I got half the water up my nose before I figured out how to run it.

I thought it was more trouble than it was worth. Just give me a plain old faucet and a clean glass and I'll get along fine.

After I'd cleaned up, I walked down the street to the Library of Congress, a great big building that took up a whole block. It took me twenty minutes to locate the office where I was supposed to go.

I walked in and stood around for a while. Phones were ringing and people were rushing around. At last a lady named Ms. Wiseman spotted me and introduced herself. She wore western boots, a skirt, and a vest over a white blouse.

I told her who I was and she smiled and said they had been expecting me. She asked if my accommodations were acceptable, and I was about to tell her about the drinking fountain when someone called her to the phone.

I couldn't help hearing the conversation. It had something to do with a horse. The guy on the other end of the line was supposed to deliver a horse.

She hung up and came over to me, shaking her head. "Mr. Erickson, didn't you tell us that you were going to do some rope tricks?"

"Well, not tricks, just a demonstration of some pasture loops and throws. I don't know anything about trick roping."

"But you need something to catch, right? We've been looking all over town for . . . what did you call it?"

"A roping dummy?"

"That's it. We can't find one. There's not a roping dummy in all of Washington, I'm sorry. But we've found a fiber glass horse that we're going to use to display a saddle. Can you rope a horse?"

"Does it have horns?"

She stared at me.

"I'm just kidding. I'll have to rope heads instead of horns, that's all."

"They're bringing over the horse. It's the best we can do. Now we have to find a saddle for it. You didn't bring your saddle, did you?"

I couldn't help smiling at the thought of me dragging my old Heiser saddle down the aisle of the Boeing 727 and trying to stuff it into the overhead luggage compartment. As dirty and beat up as that old thing was, they would have had to fumigate the plane once we got to Dulles International.

I said no, I hadn't brought my saddle.

"Well, we've got to find one." She called to a lady in another office. "Who in this city would have a saddle?"

"How about Malcolm Baldrige? Isn't he into rodeo?"

"Malcolm Baldrige! Yes, of course. I'll call his office right now."

She sprang to the phone and dialed the number of Malcolm Baldrige. I'd heard of him. He had overcome a terrible handicap to become President Reagan's Secretary of Commerce.

You see, Mr. Baldrige was known to be a roping fool, a heeler. In spite of this stain on his record, it appeared that he was going to amount to something.

Well, Ms. Wiseman had a long conversation with Mr. Baldrige's secretary. Then she hung up, clapped her hands together, and plunged into an office nearby.

"I just talked to Mack Baldrige's office. They've given us permission to use his personal roping saddle. *Mack Baldrige's saddle*! And they're sending his driver and limousine over to get us right away!"

That went over big. Everyone was happy about it. I was happy about it. Never in my life had I roped a fiber glass horse with a cabinet member's saddle on it. Tomorrow promised to be a big day.

Ms. Wiseman came out of the other office, a big smile lighting up her face. She asked me if I wanted to go with her to get the saddle.

"Sure. I'll even carry it for you."

Her smile slipped a notch or two. "No thanks. I was raised on a ranch and I can carry my own saddles. But if you want to go along for the ride, you're welcome."

"Okay."

She wanted to carry her own saddle? That was fine with me. I had dragged saddles around cow lots in three states, and I'd just about milked all the fun out of it. A few minutes later a gray Lincoln limousine pulled up in front of our building and we climbed in the back seat. The driver was wearing a chauffeur's suit and cap, just like in the movies.

We drove down one of the main streets of the city. Maybe it *was* Main Street, I don't remember the name, but it had one huge building after another. Ms. Wiseman named them for me: State Department, Treasury Department, FBI, the Smithsonian Institution, and so forth.

We pulled up to the curb in front of another huge building, this one six floors tall and a block long. It was the Department of Commerce.

We went inside and caught the elevator up. Then we walked a quarter-mile and entered the office of the Secretary of Commerce. The Secretary's secretary greeted us and told us that Mr. Baldrige was out, but we could go ahead and get his saddle.

We followed her into Mr. Baldrige's office and she led us over to the corner where his saddle sat on a wooden rack. I could tell at a glance that it was a big, heavy roping saddle with bull hide cinches and a dally horn about the size of a snubbin' post.

Sure was glad the people in Washington didn't believe in chivalry. Packing that rascal out to the car would be a chore.

Just then, who do you suppose walked in the door? Mr. Baldrige. He was a tall, thin man. Looked a little tired and pale, but he had a nice easy smile.

Ms. Wiseman began telling him about the exhibit at the Library of Congress and mentioned that I was a cowboy from Texas. All at once his eyes lit up. He heard no more about the exhibit. He said, "Come with me. I want to show you something."

He reached under a big oak table and pulled out a cardboard box and lifted out a wooden steer about three feet long. He set it out away from the table, hit a switch that made the back legs move back and forth, and handed me a little 3/16" practice rope.

Mercy! Two roping fools had met in the nation's capitol.

He built a loop in his rope and made his toss. When he got loose, I moved in and made mine. I don't know how long this went on, but I know that it might have stretched into the night if Ms. Wiseman hadn't looked at her watch and said, "We'd better get back to the Library."

Me and Mr. Baldrige exchanged smiles and coiled up our ropes. He sighed and went back to the business of running the Commerce Department, and we went back to the Library of Congress.

Well, the next day we had our program in an auditorium in the Library of Congress, and right up in front stood Trigger the Fiber Glass Horse, wearing Malcolm Baldrige's roping saddle.

He looked pretty wild, so I don't mind telling people that I roped a "wild horse" in the Library of Congress.

The scholars went first and read their papers. They were all good papers but somewhere between the Spanish Colonial Period and the Traildriving Era, my chair started getting hard.

I glanced at Brownie, an old cowboy from Louisiana who was sitting next to me, and noticed that his eyes had glazed over. In fact, they looked a lot like Trigger's eyes.

I poked him with an elbow and whispered, "Say, have you tried out that drinking fountain in your bathroom yet?"

"Shore did, and it liked to have knocked my eye out!"

I was the first of the cowboys to get up and talk. I talked about cowboying in the plains country of Texas and Oklahoma, showed a few slides my wife had taken, and ended by giving a demonstration of pasture roping techniques.

Old Trigger was so tall that I found myself throwing uphill. I missed my first heading loop (my best throw) but came back and nailed him on the second one. Then I caught him with a hoolihan, heeled him a couple of times, and was about to demonstrate an old-time forefooting loop called the Blocker, when the scholar in charge interrupted and said we'd better move along.

The scholars kept the clock, see, and controlled the microphones. I had a feeling they didn't trust me or Brownie or Leon Coffee or Les Stewart with that job.

Les Stewart was a rancher from Nevada, and he talked about the buckaroo approach to cowboying. He and I were the dally men in the group, while Brownie and Leon Coffee represented the hard-and-fast point of view.

It didn't take us long to get into a fight about which was better, tie or dally. Those tie-solid boys were stubborn and muleheaded. Me and Les Stewart were too, but at least we were *right*.

One of the things Les said about dally ropers was that they *never* tie a knot in the home-end of their ropes, because a knot can pull your hand into the dallies.

I thought that was very interesting, and for the rest of our time on stage, I kept my hand around the knot in the home-end of my rope. I didn't want to tell the audience how many times I'd missed my wraps and managed to hang on to my cow only because of that knot.

Brownie sang a few cowboy songs and then Leon did some rope tricks. As you may know, Leon made his living as a PRCA clown and bullfighter, and you wouldn't expect a guy like that to know much about the rope. But he did a trick that sure impressed me. He started out spinning the rope. Then he stepped inside the loop, spun it up over his head, brought it around to the right, and danged if he didn't end up by heeling Trigger the Wild Fiber Glass Horse!

I was kind of glad the people in the audience didn't know anything about roping, because Coffee had just made my little exhibition of pasture roping look pretty sad. And him being a hard-and-fast man on top of that.

Well, that ended the symposium. We dally boys made peace with the tie-solid boys and said our good-bys, and before long we were all flying back to where we came from.

Oh, I never did finish the story about Mr. Baldrige's saddle. When it was time for us to leave the Secretary's office, Ms. Wiseman went over to fetch the saddle which she had already told me she could carry because she grew up on a ranch.

She lifted it off the rack, held it there for a second, and put it back down. Then she turned to me and said, "Oh, I guess I'll let you carry it this time."

Which just goes to prove that if the saddle's heavy enough, there's still a place for a gentleman in this old world.

Chapter Eleven

No Man's Land — And Why

The Oklahoma Panhandle was a stepchild from the beginning.

In the 19th century, when the United States was expanding westward, national attention was fixed on the slavery question, the Indian problem, and routes the railroads would follow.

When Texas and Kansas were admitted into the Union and their boundaries established, the leaders of our nation made a slight miscalculation: they overlooked a strip of land 168 miles long and 35 miles wide and left 5800 square miles of land dangling between Kansas, Colorado, New Mexico, Texas, and Indian Territory.

It was neither a state nor a territory. It belonged to no one. United States courts and marshals didn't have authority to function within its boundaries. No one did. It became a legal and administrative vacuum, appropriately called No Man's Land, and by the 1880s it was drawing outlaws, horse thieves, and scoundrels, who came like hogs to a mudhole.

Respectable citizens also came, and to protect themselves against the lawless element, they established vigilante groups. A member of one of these groups once addressed an unsavory character in this manner:

"We'll convert you and make you a Christian, by God, if we have to hang you!"

It was not an idle threat. Before law and order arrived in No Man's Land, the hemp committees had decorated several cotton-woods with outlaws.

In 1890 under the administration of President Harrison, No Man's Land was annexed to the new Oklahoma Territory, which ended its status as a legal non-entity. In 1907, when Congress worked up enough courage to admit Oklahoma into the Family, the Neutral Strip tagged along.

And ever since, it has been known as the Oklahoma Pan-handle.

Today (1977), the Panhandle is more or less part of the Unit-ed States, but to those of us who live here, the feeling that we are stepchildren persists. This is probably a common feeling among people who dwell in these geographical oddities known as "pan-handles."

A better term might be "tail of the dog." We are far from the heart, far from the head, the last to be scratched, and the first to be stepped on.

The sense of isolation one feels in the Oklahoma Panhan-dle is not imaginary. In the first place, we are right in the middle of Southwestern culture and commerce — right *square* in the mid-dle. A day's drive in any direction will bring you to a museum, a modern airport, a department store, or a good library.

A visitor to the Panhandle once mentioned this to a native cowboy. "Say, you people aren't far from the boondocks, are you?"

"Nope," said the cowboy, "we've got two of them in the south part of the county."

Also contributing to our isolation is the fact that, although we are Oklahomans by virtue of taxation and vote, we are joined to the mother state by a tenuous 35 mile border, which means that if God ever tries to pick up Oklahoma by its handle, the state will break into two pieces.

Any carpenter could tell you that Oklahoma was poorly designed. You simply couldn't put enough nails and glue on the Beaver County-Harper County line to overcome its structural weakness.

The Panhandle has approximately 410 miles of outside border. Of that sum, we share 160 with Texas, 115 with Kansas, 55 with Colorado, 35 with New Mexico, and 35 with Oklahoma.

Hence, by the verdict of geography, we are mostly Texan, partly Kansan and Coloradoan, and no more Oklahoman than we are New Mexican. You could say that we missed being someone else by a very slim margin.

One result of this is that it's almost impossible to get a reliable weather report for the Panhandle. On an average day, you can pick up one Oklahoma station on your radio: KGYN in Guymon. The rest of the broadcasts come out of Kansas and Texas.

If you listen to a Texas station, the weather report will come out of Amarillo, some 200 miles to the south. If you listen to a Kansas station, their weather forecast comes out of Garden City, a hundred miles to the north.

If you listen to the Oklahoma station, you will hear a weather report which probably originated in Oklahoma City, 250 miles to the east. Once again, we're right in the middle of things — about fifty miles beyond anyone's ability to forecast the weather.

What makes this condition bearable is that Panhandle weather is unpredictable anyway, and the National Weather Service merely serves up daily proof of it. In these parts, listening to the weather report is a habit and a form of entertainment. No one really expects to learn anything.

This can be annoying, but it's nothing compared with the telephone system.

The Oklahoma Panhandle has what surely must be the most bizarre and complicated phone system in the Western Hemisphere. In this age of communications satellites, it is easier to place a call to Hong Kong than to complete a call from one point in the Panhandle to another, especially if you're calling from ranch to ranch.

Let's look at the situation in Beaver County, one of three counties in the Panhandle. Beaver County is approximately 55 miles from east to west and 35 miles from north to south. It is primarily a rural area, with Beaver City, the county seat, as the only town of any size — about 2500 souls.

The other communities in the county — Forgan, Turpin, Bryan's Corner, Balko, Elmwood, Knowles, Gate, and Slapout — vary in size from tiny to microscopic.

Beaver County, with a combined population of about 10,000, is not serviced by one telephone company, but by three: General Telephone, Southwestern Bell, and the Panhandle Telephone Cooperative.

The county has been chopped up into no less than *eight* separate telephone exchanges: Balko, Beaver, Bryan's Corner, Floris, Forgan, Gate, Logan, and Turpin. The one exception to this occurs in the Forgan-Floris area, where the 330 people on the Forgan exchange have the pleasure of calling the 140 people on the Floris exchange toll-free, and vice versa.

This multiple exchange system creates several problems. The first is that one's phone bill is made up almost entirely of long distance calls to people who don't live a long distance away.

The second is that, before you can find someone's phone number, you have to know first what exchange his phone comes out of.

The third is that there is no logic to the system.

Example: If a Family X gets its mail from the Knowles post office, sends its children to school in Forgan, and attends church in Beaver, what is their telephone exchange?

Answer: Gate.

The fourth problem is that the three phone companies and eight county exchanges don't combine their listings. There is no single telephone directory for Beaver County. There are three or four phone books, and to find a number, you must have them all.

To understand just how complicated life can be under this so-called system, let us take a closer look at the telephone in my house, here on the Beaver River.

We live on a ranch 18 crow-miles and 13 cattle guards east of Beaver. We are in the Beaver school district, our mail comes out of the Knowles post office, and we are on the Logan telephone exchange.

Logan? What is Logan? Logan is a rural post office out in the middle of nowhere. I have never seen Logan and don't know exactly where it is, only that it's somewhere on the other side of the river.

I have no idea why there is a telephone exchange out of Logan or why we are on it.

All right, since I work on a ranch, let's suppose that I need to contact eight or nine of the neighbors to let them know that we'll need them for our spring roundup. Fool that I am, I decide to use the telephone instead of a signal fire.

I begin by calling Stanley, who lives five miles up the river, who is also on the Logan exchange, and who is one of the few neighbors we can call toll-free.

Next, I call Lloyd, whose house sits fifty feet to the north of Stanley's house but whose phone is on the Beaver exchange. The houses are fifty feet apart, yet they are on different exchanges and a call from one house to the other is long distance.

G.L.Holmes

Now I try to call David, who lives eight miles north, near the town of Knowles. I thumb through my directories, looking for the Knowles exchange. Ten minutes later, I have made a discovery: there is no Knowles exchange.

I check the Logan listings. Nope. I check the Forgan listings. Nope. David is on the *Gate* exchange.

Then I make another discovery. My directory from the Panhandle Telephone Cooperative has listings for Balko, Bryan's Corner, Logan, and Turpin, but not Gate. My Southwestern Bell directory has listings for Forgan and Floris, but no Gate. My General Telephone book has listings for Beaver, but no Gate.

All these cursed phone books and I still can't find a listing in Gate. My gosh, he just lives up the road!

I skip David and go on to Darrell, who lives nine miles east of Gate but whose phone comes out of Laverne, and I don't have a Laverne phone book.

Then I try to find the number for Jake, who lives seven miles west of Beaver but whose phone is not listed in the Beaver directory. I have to make two long distance calls to find out that Jake's phone is listed in the Balko exchange.

I should have known. Since Jake gets his mail from the Beaver post office, sends his children to the Beaver schools, and lives just a whoop and a holler outside of Beaver, it stands to reason that his phone would be out of Balko.

All these calls were made to people who lived within thirty miles of my home, and all but one were long distance. But that's not the end of the complications. When you direct-dial a number, your chances of getting the call through the first time are only about one in four.

If it happens to be raining, your chances drop to one in twelve. And by the time you get through, someone on the party line wants to use the phone.

And whatever the weather, you're assured of a bad connection, with a wonderful variety of electronic noises, ranging from ordinary static which blots out the voice on the other end, to a high-pitched squeal which goes through your ear like a red-hot knitting needle.

Oh well. Such is life in the Oklahoma Panhandle. In the 1880s no one would claim this strip of land. Today, we're beginning to understand why.

Chapter Twelve

Working With Jake

In 1979 I was cowboying on the old Otto Barby ranch along the Beaver River in the Oklahoma Panhandle.

The original ranch had spread across something like 100,000 acres of fine sand hill and river bottom country, but by the time I got there the Old Gentleman had died and the ranch had been split up among his heirs.

Now, instead of one huge Barby ranch, there were six smaller outfits covering the same amount of country. Since all of us were out in an isolated part of Beaver County, we neighbored back and forth and swapped out work.

Our nearest neighbor to the west was Leland Barby's Three Cross Ranch. The foreman of that outfit was named Jake Parker, and I always looked forward to working with him.

He was an older man, maybe 45 or 50, and one of the best cowboys in a country that had produced some great ones. He was tough enough to work fourteen-hour days, but he also had a gentle, easy-going nature, and even when the work was hard and the days were long, we had fun.

One morning in the spring of 1979, I hauled my horse over to the Three Cross to help Jake and Leland shuffle some cattle around. When I pulled in at the barn, Jake and Leland came down from the house, where they had been drinking coffee and planning out the day's work.

Jake handed me a little package of something wrapped up in tin foil. "Sue baked a cake this morning and wanted you to have a piece of it."

I had just finished a big breakfast of venison and eggs and wasn't particularly hungry, so I slipped the cake into a pocket of my down-filled vest.

That was nice of Sue. She and Leland had just gotten married a few weeks before, and she knew how much we cowboys admired good home-built desserts. Obviously she was trying to make a good impression, just as we cowboys were anxious to make a good impression on her.

From now on, she would be cheffing the roundup meals on the Three Cross and we all wanted to stay on her good side.

We saddled up and spent the morning separating cattle in the meadow pastures near headquarters. Around 12:30 we rode back to the barn, fed the horses, and went up to the house for lunch.

After the meal, Sue brought out a long cake pan and started cutting the cake. I told her she didn't need to cut a piece for me because I hadn't eaten the piece she'd given me that morning. I unwrapped the tin foil and stared at the contents. At first glance, it didn't look much like cake. At second glance, it still didn't. In fact, it looked a whole lot like three lumps of horse manure.

I could see that Parker was about to rip the buttons off his vest, trying to hold back his laughter.

So! It was all clear now. Sue had fallen in with a bad crowd and was already playing pranks, even though she had only been on the river for a few weeks.

She delivered plates of cake to Jake and Leland. I waited for her to bring me one, but she didn't. She was going to string the joke out, I could see that.

"How's the cake, John?"

"It tastes kind of funny."

She stared at me. "Is something wrong with it, really?"

"Yep. I think you put too much baking powder in it."

Say, she was doing a great job of acting. That shocked expression on her face looked pretty authentic, and I noticed that she had even managed to blush. Jake and Leland had taught her well, and she was going to milk the joke down to the last squirt.

She came over to my place at the table, snatched up the tin foil, and took it back to the counter.

I glanced around the table. Parker was about to herniate himself, trying to hold back his laughter, but . . . that was odd. Leland wasn't laughing. If I hadn't known better, I might have thought that he was . . . well, embarrassed. Or mad.

Then Sue let out a gasp. *"Horse manure!"* She spun around. *"Jake Parker, did you do this?"*

By that time Parker had stopped trying to hold it back and was half-way out of his chair. In other words, yes, he had done it.

Come to find out, Sue and Leland hadn't been in on the prank at all. Sue had given Parker the piece of cake that morning and had asked him to give it to me, only he had eaten it himself and had replaced it with the horse biscuits.

Sue had thought I was insulting her cake, and I suppose that Leland thought I had either lost my manners or my mind.

It took poor Sue several days to recover, and every time someone mentioned "cake" she would start blushing again. I don't think she ever trusted a cowboy after that.

Jake seldom missed a chance to pull a prank on someone, but he was pretty serious when it came to cow work. He didn't believe in chousing cattle or abusing horses, and while he loved to rope as much as we younger guys did, he didn't take his rope down until it was necessary.

When he did, he would stick it on anything that wore hair, and it was always a fast, clean job. One loop was all he ever needed.

I recall one incident when all the foolishness went out of Jake. It involved a horse named Boston Blackie.

One morning in May, not long after the famous Cake Incident, I went over to the Three Cross to help Jake and his nephew, Bud Parker, round up a bunch of yearling heifers.

I was riding a sorrel mare named Ginger, and Jake rode a big dun gelding named Buck. He had picked up Buck from a horse trader and had made an honest horse out of him. Jake and I were well-mounted for the day's work, but Bud, who was 16 and a little green, was having problems with Boston Blackie.

Blackie was near the bottom of the Three Cross's work string. He had papers and was supposed to have been bred right, but he had a hard mouth and a silly disposition, and it seemed that nobody ever got around to riding him.

Jake had put his nephew on Blackie, in hopes that a few wet blankets and some time in the pasture would settle him down. But all morning he had been watching the horse, and he didn't like what he saw.

We gathered the heifers and penned them in a set of steel landing-mat corrals, and all at once Blackie started acting silly, as though he'd never been in a corral before. He danced around and had rollers in his nose, and when Bud spurred him, he reared up.

Just for a moment there, it appeared that he would go over backwards and land on top of Bud.

Now, Jake had broke and trained horses all his life, and he was especially good with young horses. He was able to see the world as they might see it, and I had often admired his patience in dealing with them. He could forgive a colt for making a mistake, and I had never seen him lose his temper.

But Boston Blackie wasn't a colt. He knew exactly what he was doing. He had a boy up in the saddle and he was pulling a cheap trick to intimidate him.

Boy, let me tell you, old Parker flew out of his saddle and yelled, "Let me have that jackass!" You'd have thought that the neighborhood bully had picked a fight with his nephew.

Blackie snorted and pawed the ground. Bud bailed out and Jake took the reins. I stepped off my mare and dropped her reins. I knew Parker was fixing to have a showdown with Blackie, and I wanted to be in a position to help him if he got into a wreck.

To tell you the truth, I was scared for Jake. You could see in Blackie's eyes that he had bad things on his mind, and going over backwards in a landing-mat corral was about as bad a thing as I could imagine.

The thought of a crushed pelvis had always given me a bad case of the horrors, whether it was mine or someone else's.

Jake stepped up into the saddle and took hold of the reins. "What do you mean, trying to go over backwards with a kid! You just try that with me, old pup!"

Blackie danced around and humped up his back, and every time he made a false move, Jake ran some iron into his shoulder. It appeared to me that Jake was *trying* to get him to go over backwards.

For several minutes I didn't know what would happen, whether Blackie would blow the cork or if he would take the scolding. But one thing was clear: Jake had no intention of backing down. He would either win the argument or get himself hurt.

This should have been a solemn occasion, and in one way it was. But in another way it came close to comedy, because once Parker lost his temper, he started talking in a squeaky falsetto. He sounded just like an old woman, and I could hardly keep from laughing.

"Acting up with a kid and trying to scare him!" he squeaked. "You old fool, I ought to whip your ears off! Now, you try that with me and see what happens!"

Blackie hopped up on his back legs, while Bud and I watched with big eyes and wondered if Jake was going to get himself smashed and tried to keep from laughing at his old woman's voice.

The tension ran high for several minutes, and then Blackie quit. He had gone to the brink and had decided that Jake wasn't whistling Dixie.

Bud climbed back into the saddle — looking a little pale, I thought — and he had no more trouble out of Boston Blackie that day.

As we were crossing the Beaver River, heading for the Duck Pond Creek pasture, I asked Jake if he had really wanted the horse to go over with him. When he said yes, I asked him what he would have done.

"Well, when he starts going up and back, you kick out of the stirrups, push yourself over the back of the saddle, and pull him over backwards with the reins. Then, when you've got him on the ground, there's things you can do that'll make him wish he wasn't there. You can make a Christian out of a horse pretty quick."

"Holy smokes, Parker, what happens if you don't get out of the saddle in time?"

"Well, then the horse might make a Christian out of *you*."

He went on to say that he hadn't used that technique in several years and that he wasn't as quick as he used to be, and he was kind of glad Blackie hadn't tested him out.

I was kind of glad too, since I would have been the one who would have had to scrape Parker off the landing mats and haul him over thirteen cattle guards to town.

Chapter Thirteen

Pulling Pranks On Hobart

Hobart Hall was an old cowboy I worked with up on the Beaver River in 1978-79. He must have been around sixty when I met him. My first impression of him was that he was an old grouch. He went around with a scowl on his face and talked in a gruff tone of voice. But I soon found out that he had a good heart and a boyish sense of humor.

Another thing I learned about Hobart was that he was goosey. Now, most people will jump when they get poked in the ribs or goosed with a stick, but Hobart's goosiness was of a different order of magnitude. When goosed, he became dangerous.

In my first month with the roundup crew, Jake Parker warned me about Hobart. "If you goose him and you're standing too close, he's just liable to turn around and slug you."

"*Slug* you? Why would he do that?"

Jake shook his head. "They tell me that he served on submarines in World War II and the Germans dropped a bunch of depth charges on them. Ever since, he's been goosey."

Well, that still didn't make any sense to me. What did depth charges have to do with being goosed on dry land? Parker had told me all he knew about the causes of goosiness and he couldn't satisfy my curiosity on the subject. But he told me a story that illustrated just how goosey Hobart was.

Lloyd Barby was one of our neighbors on the river and we often worked cattle with him. Lloyd was a grown man but had the heart of a little boy when it came to pulling pranks. He just loved to pull pranks on the cowboys, and goosing Hobart was one of his favorite pastimes

One fall during the shipping season, a new man came to work on the crew, and it turned out that he was just as goosey as Hobart. If you slipped up behind either one of them and poked him, he would turn wrongside out and start slapping or slugging anyone who happened to be close by.

The crew had gathered a pasture, penned the cattle, and separated the cows from the calves. Now came the slow work of running the calves across the scales and loading them into cattle trucks.

Hobart and this other fellow were standing next to each other in the middle of an alley. They were talking and killing time. Since they had been separating cattle, each one was armed with a three-foot piece of windmill rod.

Lloyd slipped up on their blind side and goosed both of them at the same time, and then he ran. Both men jumped and hollered, and they started whacking on each other with the windmill rods!

Jake said that if they hadn't been wearing heavy winter coats, they might have beat each other to death.

Lloyd wasn't the only man on the crew who pulled pranks on Hobart. We all did. I think Hobart enjoyed being teased by the younger men, and he was quite capable of turning it around and taking care of himself, as we shall see.

I remember one day in the spring when our crew was working on the old Ralph Barby place, on the river south of Knowles. We had gathered a pasture of cows and calves south of the river, pushed them across the river, and penned them in a big set of shipping pens at headquarters.

As I recall, the calves in this bunch were late calves that had been too small to ship in the fall, and Darrell Cox, the Open A foreman, wanted to wean them and haul them to another place.

So we stripped off the calves and started loading them in our stock trailers. We must have had six or seven trailers there that day, and we needed every one of them to haul the cattle.

Hobart had his old red four-wheel drive Ford pickup hitched to a 16-foot trailer, and when it came his turn, he backed up to the loading chute, parked it, and went back to the crowding pen to help with the loading.

We had a surplus of cowboys that day, which meant that some of us had nothing to do but stand around thinking of mischief. Pat Mason and I fell into that category, and when we saw Hobart leave his rig unattended, we looked at each other and sprang into action.

Pat slipped into the cab, turned on the windshield wipers and the heater fan, and turned the volume knob on the radio as high as it would go. Then he slipped the four-wheel drive transfer lever into the neutral position.

While he was doing that, I found a one gallon paint bucket and wired it to the front bumper, so that it would drag the ground. Then we took cover behind a stock trailer to watch the show.

Old Hobart climbed into his pickup and his mind was miles away. He started the motor and the instant his fingers released the key, the radio blared, dust and alfalfa leaves fogged out of the defroster vents, and the windshield wipers went to flapping.

It startled him so badly that he almost tore the steering wheel off its column, but he composed himself and decided that he was going to be mature about it. He knew someone was waiting for him to respond and he wasn't going to give us that satisfaction.

So he threw the pickup in gear, gunned the motor, and eased off the clutch. By this time several of the boys had joined us and we had let them in on our joke.

The pickup didn't move. By this time Hobart was talking to himself. He turned down the radio, shut off the heater fan and the windshield wipers, and ground off half a pound of gear metal shifting the transfer lever back up into two-wheel drive.

He gunned the motor and spun his tires and pulled away from the loading chute, with the paint can making a wonderful clatter.

He drove past us and saw us slapping our knees and holding our sides with laughter. He gave us an evil glare with his old lizard eyes and said something. His window was rolled up, so we couldn't hear him, but we read his lips.

I can't tell you his exact words because they weren't very mature.

He went clattering down the road and never did stop to take off the paint can.

That afternoon, we gathered the Rutherford pasture, which was just south of the Ralph Barby place. This was a typical Beaver River pasture, with high sand hills on the north end and heavy tamarack brush along the river.

Our objective for the drive was to throw the cattle out of the hills, take them through the tamaracks and across the river, and drive them to another pasture two miles to the south.

Taking cattle through the tamaracks was a risky proposition because some of those old sisters were "brushy" and weren't fond of the idea of leaving. The brush was so heavy in spots that you couldn't ride a horse through it, or if you tried, you ran the risk of getting stabbed and your clothes torn off.

I had lost a good spur that way. The brush had torn it off my boot.

Well, we didn't have any trouble flushing the cattle out of the hills, but once we got them into the brush, we started earning our wages. Following deer trails through the tamaracks and checking the ground for fresh cow tracks, we pushed everything south toward the river.

Kary Cox and I ran into each other on the north bank. Each of us had followed a bunch through the brush, and now we threw them together and tried to put them into the water. It wasn't very deep, a foot or less, and after much whipping and spurring and riding back and forth, we got several of the cows to leave the north bank and venture out into the water.

But then two big sappy calves whirled around and headed back into the brush. We couldn't stop them and they disappeared into the tamarack jungle.

They split and we knew it was to bring out the "Long Arm of the Cowboy." We took down our ropes. I must admit that this wasn't exactly a dreaded moment. All of us younger guys on the crew were a little rope-crazy, and going after the wild ones was good sport to us.

Kary went after one and I went after the other.

It turned into a wild ride through the brush. One minute I would have my calf in sight and would build to him with a hungry loop, but then he would dive into some thick brush and I would lose him. Then I would have to follow him by sound, picking my way around the heavier brush without getting my loop snagged or my eyes poked out.

As long as he kept moving and rattling the brush, I had a chance of finding him. If he ever stopped, I would lose him.

I followed him for half a mile or so. Several times I rode onto him in a little clearing, but somehow I ran out of clear space before I could get off a shot.

Then I popped out of the brush and saw him up ahead. I could tell that he was getting tired. I nudged Calipso with the spurs and we went after him. This time I got off a throw just before he hit the brush. The loop settled around his neck and I dallied up.

I was feeling pretty proud of myself, but then I noticed that my head felt a little drafty. Somewhere during the chase, I had lost my $40 black Resistol hat.

I glanced around, trying to remember where I had been. I had no idea. The only landmarks in that stretch of brush were brush and more brush. Even if I had known the approximate location where the hat had come off, I doubt that I could have found it.

So I had just paid forty bucks for the honor of roping one of the Open A's calves, and forty bucks amounted to about 8% of my monthly wages. Pretty expensive fun.

I got behind the calf, slapped the rope across his back, and pointed him toward the river. We picked our way through the tamaracks. By this time, the rest of the crew was on the other side of the river, driving the main herd south toward Mexico Creek. I was all alone.

But then we came to a little clearing in the brush, and to my complete astonishment, I saw a man sitting on a paint horse. He had one leg thrown over the fork of his saddle and he was smoking a cigarette. On his head, he wore *two* hats, a gray one with a black one fitted on top of it.

It was Hobart Hall, and the second hat he wore was my black Resistol.

"Did you lose something?" he asked.

"What the heck are you doing out here?"

"Looking for strays, same as you. I seen you go flying past and thought maybe you'd lost something."

"I sure did, and I'm mighty proud of you for finding it. I was wondering where I could come up with $40 to replace it."

He gave me an evil grin. "You can have it back for five. Ain't you the same little smart aleck who tied that paint can to my pickup?"

"Well . . . uh . . . I think that was Pat Mason. Or Kary. Might have been David."

"It was *you*, and it'll cost you five bucks to get your hat back."

"Now Hobart, what's done is done. It's not good to carry a grudge."

He parked the cigarette under his lip and snapped his fingers. "Five bucks or it's my hat."

"I don't have five bucks."

"In that case, you'd better confess your sins and tell me how sorry you are for booby-trapping my pickup."

So I confessed, told him how sorry I was, and promised never to do pull childish pranks again. He grinned through it all. Oh, he loved it!

When I was done, he pitched me my hat. "There. Now see if you can keep it on your head." As we rode toward the river, he went on grumbling. "Danged kids these days. You teach 'em to ride a horse and then you have to follow 'em around to pick up their clothes. Now, when I was your age . . ."

Well, I'd gotten my hat back, but by the time Hobart got finished with me, forty bucks for a new hat looked pretty cheap.

Chapter Fourteen

Selling Beef In A Negligee

I went to the livestock auction yesterday. Fifty cents a pound would have bought anything but the auctioneer. Everything was down: cows, calves, stockers, feeders, horses, saddles, goats.

This cattle market went to the cellar a month ago and kept going. At the same time, everything we buy is going up: pickups, gas, cottonseed, lumber, bolts, windmill parts, and pie. We've got to do something to turn this cattle business around.

They tell me the problem with our market is that we've produced too many cattle. We've got to get the numbers down before the price can go up.

I've tried to do my part. Our deep freeze is so full of cripples and bloaters, we can barely shut the lid. Fifty-four cubic feet of grass-fed hamburger.

But a guy can only eat so much beef. Three times a day is about all I can stand. I hate to admit it, but every now and then I get a craving for a peanut butter and jelly sandwich.

No, we can't eat our way out of this bad cattle market, and that's why I was glad to read about these new beef promotions. Some of the cattlemen's organizations have started running ads — magazines, newspapers, radio, tv, the whole shebang.

They've hired movie stars to give their confessionals: "I eat beef because it makes me healthy and beautiful." And, "I eat beef because it's a good bargain."

That's a good start, but it seems to me they're missing the boat on those ads. They're too timid. Twenty years ago, you could have sold a product by pointing out that it was good for you and that it was priced right.

But today? Uh uh. You know what sells products today? A three-letter word that begins with S and ends with X. That's right, and if you don't believe it, just start paying attention to the ads and what they're *really* selling. It ain't soap or spaghetti.

Here's a lesson on how to sell cars. These examples come from family magazines that don't deal in racy material:

1. "The Capri Sport Coupe is the first sexy European under $2400."

2. "Buick introduces automobiles to light your fire."

3. "The Toyota Corona Hardtop is much like a beautiful woman. Vivacious. Impetuous. Unpredictable."

Now fellers, if a Toyota can be like a beautiful woman, why can't a cow? At least a cow's *alive* and has legs and a head.

And if a car can light your fire, why can't a pot roast? And if there's really something sexy about an imported sports car, maybe there's something sexy about steaks and stew meat.

The advertising people are selling us cars and toothpaste and chewing tobacco wrapped up in a negligee, so it seems only fair for us to turn around and sell them beef the same way. If people are fool enough to believe that a car is like a beautiful woman, the field is wide open for beef.

Now, I admit that there's something a little weird about the whole idea, and if you think too long about what's really being said in the ads, it makes you think that children shouldn't be allowed to see them.

I mean, I took enough biology to know about birds and bees and boys and girls, and there was nothing in our books about Toyota Corona Hardtops. I sure wouldn't want my kids to marry one of them.

But that kind of advertising seems to work, so what are we waiting for?

"The Beef Industry Council introduces the first sexy pot roast that will light your fire. Much more like a beautiful woman than either pork or chicken or automobiles. Vivacious. Impetuous. Unpredictable."

I think that's a winner. The next thing we ought to do is to come up with a pair sexy posthole diggers. The guy who comes up with that one should be elected president of something.

Chapter Fifteen

Cultured Cows

Have you heard about the experiment they ran down at A & M? Two professors, Dr. Ridiculous and Dr. Sublime, set out to make a breed of *cultured cows*.

Yes sir. Cultured cows. Their idea was that instead of breeding for the usual things — resistance to heat and insects, bigger frame, better rustling ability, color, milking, eye pigmentation, easy of calving, and so forth — they would breed for *intelligence*.

As they said in their literature, "Since the dawn of time, the bovine animal has been plagued by one major flaw: stupidity. Our studies have convinced us that an intelligent cow, properly trained and directed, will make intelligent decisions, and that intelligent decisions will result in healthier animals, better conversion of forage to beef, heavier calves at weaning time, and more dollars for the rancher."

In 1980 they went all over the world shopping for foundation stock. They didn't want your ordinary dumb cow. They wanted the smartest cows in the whole world, cows that could be taught and educated, cows that could be taught to *think* and *communicate*.

They found them in a mountain village in Austria and shipped them back to Texas. Thirty head of the smartest cows in the world. They made your ordinary Texas sookie look like a moron.

First thing they did was to work out a system of communication, and after a year they found that these cows could understand about a hundred words and signs.

When the scientists said it was time to eat, the cows ate. When the scientists said it was time to wean a calf, they'd kick off the calf. When the scientists said it was time to breed back, they'd go hunt up the bull.

By 1984 the system was working like a Swiss watch. The steer calves were getting five cents over market price, heifers started at a thousand bucks apiece, and the bull calves were being sold for outrageous prices.

There were still wealthy oil men in Texas at that time.

The scientists had made their point. Cultured cows could make money. They were all set to establish the Cultured Cow Breeders Association . . . when problems developed.

One day in the spring of 1985, one of the cows let it be known (through signs and swishes of her tail) that she resented having to walk around the pasture looking for grass. That was okay for ordinary dumb cows, but she expected better.

The resentment spread and other cows voiced the same opinion. They wanted an air conditioned barn, piped-in music, and a good grade of feed brought to the trough.

Well, the scientists themselves had educated these cows so they had to respect their opinions. They ran their numbers on a computer and decided that it was a pretty good idea. It would work.

But then the cows had another gripe. They didn't think a cultured cow should have to nurse her own calf. She had better things to do, which brought up another gripe: they didn't have anything to do, standing around the barn all day, and they were getting bored.

They wanted television.

Well, this seemed a bit much to the scientists, but they ran the numbers on a spreadsheet and, would you believe it? The figures showed that by lowering the cows' energy requirements, they could save enough on the feed bills to pay for nurse cows and television sets!

All went well until last February, when the cows brought up the subject of birth control.

Birth control? The scientists put that one into the computer and it came up with a two-word answer: "Ho, ho."

It would never work. The research team put the nix on it and the cows went on strike. They refused to do anything that interfered with their television programs, which included everything that ordinary cows do. They refused to eat, drink, breed, nurse, and graze.

And so it was that this noble experiment ended in failure, and we will never see the Cultured Cow Breeders Association. The animals in the Cultured Cow Foundation Herd are now appearing in supermarkets all over Texas, Oklahoma, and New Mexico.

You will find them in the meat section, listed under "Hamburger."

Chapter Sixteen

Free Enterprise Isn't Dead

You often hear it said these days that the spirit of free enterprise is dead in our country, small business doesn't have a chance, big corporations are the only ones who can survive, and so forth.

I don't think that's quite right. I've had a little experience in the small business field, and there's no question in my mind that free enterprise is alive and well.

People who are willing to work hard and take a few chances can make it, especially if they're involved in crime.

The picture isn't nearly as bright for someone who tries to make a living running a grocery store, cafe, farm, book store, or small town newspaper. Things are getting pretty tough in those lines, but in the criminal world, the business climate is great. In fact, it may be the last bastion of the free enterprise system.

Criminals have some tremendous advantages over the mom and pop store on the corner. Criminals never have to deal with the State Comptroller's office. When they start up their businesses, they don't receive a 50 page book called "Your New Business and the Texas Sales Tax," which begins with this cheerful greeting:

"Dear Taxpayer: If you operate a business in the State of Texas, you will be dealing directly with the Texas Sales and Use Tax. You may also be subject to the Franchise Tax."

Criminals don't pay Texas Sales and Use Tax. They don't pay the Franchise Tax. Best of all, they don't have to read the book.

Criminals don't have to consult accountants or psychiatrists around April 15. They don't have to keep envelopes stuffed with receipts and cancelled checks. They don't have to borrow money to pay their income tax because they don't pay income tax.

There may be some argument about whether or not crime pays, but there's no question that it's tax-exempt.

If a criminal needs an employee in his business, he just goes out and hires one — no Social Security mess, no workman's compensation or liability insurance, no unemployment payments, no income tax withholding.

The criminal has only one thing to fear from the law: arrest. And there's a good chance he'll never be caught, let alone prosecuted and sentenced. On the other hand, mom and pop have much to fear from the law: hateful letters, harassment, investigation, audit, arrest, prosecution, imprisonment, seizure of assets, and financial ruin.

The mom and pop business may be obsolete in our day. Certainly the tax advantages lie on the other side of the law. After all, it's much easier to impose taxes on honest citizens than on gangsters who don't play by the rules.

So there you are. Free enterprise is far from dead. It's alive and thriving. Fortunes are still being made and the American dream is still being dreamed. But it helps if your business is robbery, burglary, or drug smuggling.

Chapter Seventeen
Animal Liberation

There for a while, I thought we'd liberated just about every oppressed minority group in the country. During the sixties and seventies, minority groups came out of nowhere, demanding recognition and their constitutional rights.

One of the biggest shocks of that period came when women, who are a majority group, became a minority group. Another shock came in 1978 when an Australian professor named Peter Singer brought out a book called *Animal Liberation: A New Ethics For Our Treatment of Animals*. I was cowboying in Oklahoma at the time, and I thought Professor Singer was writing humor. I should have known better. Back then, universities didn't allow humor because it wasn't considered serious enough.

He wasn't kidding. "Our attitudes to members of other species," he wrote, "are a form of prejudice no less objectionable than prejudice about a person's race or sex."

He called this discrimination "speciesism."

Let's see: racism, sexism, ageism, and now speciesism. Just when you think you've adjusted to the modern world and cleaned yourself up, a new -ism comes along and you've got to examine your soul again.

All right, *speciesism*. Is there anything to the charge that we humans discriminate against animals? In a word, yes.

I have never allowed my horses to saddle me. I have never even asked their opinion about it.

I have never butchered my children or the neighbors' children when we needed meat. We cling to the idea that eating beef is better in the long run, although I must say that on a few occasions the thought of . . . never mind. They're nice kids most of the time.

I have never offered to lay eggs for our chickens. I wouldn't know how to lay an egg, and I really don't want to learn. Besides, I find the idea of eating grasshoppers repulsive.

Yes, I confess to having made sweeping generalizations about cattle as a group. I have said on many occasions, often in a loud voice, that cattle are stupid — all cattle, not just a few individuals. That's probably a sign of speciesism. And yes, I've discriminated against our dogs. They have offered to run the ranch for me many times and I've turned them down. Do I have any scientific proof that I'm smarter than they are? Not really. And, to tell you the truth, I've wondered about it from time to time.

Sounds pretty bad so far, but there's more. The public image of ranch animals is patronizing and degrading. As things stand today, it would be virtually impossible for a school child to believe that a cow, horse, sheep, goat, chicken, or hog could be elected President of the United States.

Equal employment opportunities? They don't exist for ranch animals. The Department of Agriculture, which keeps statistics on the farm and ranch industry, has never elevated a single farm or ranch animal to a position of authority. Most universities have never admitted a farm or ranch animal as a student. No labor union in the country offers a training program for farm or ranch animals.

Voting rights? They don't exist.

You add all this up and it makes you think there really is such a thing as "speciesism." Every day in this land of the free, we Americans make decisions that are based on the notion that animals are animals and people are people.

Professor Singer is right, and I think someone should recognize his contribution to knowledge by making him an Honorary Donkey.

I wonder if the founders of this nation had any idea that their noble experiment was going to cause so much trouble. Surely not.

Chapter Eighteen

Good Management

Lonnie lived down along the creek and he was a pretty good operator. He ran good cows, worked hard, and tried to stay on top of the market.

A couple of years ago in October, he figured it was about time to round up and ship his calves. But when he checked the market against his expenses, he calculated that if he sold right then, he'd lose $10 a head straight across.

Well, he wasn't going to have any of that, so he held on to his calves, leased some wheat pasture, and ran them all winter. By the time they reached feeder weight, he figured the market would come back.

But come April, the market was even lower. He figured up labor, expenses, pasture lease, medicine, and death loss, and saw that if he sold, he'd lose 25 bucks a head.

Couldn't do that, so he just got mad and hauled them to the feedlot. He'd feed 'em out himself. By the time they had a good finish on them, the market would be back in the real world.

It was a nice set of calves and they did real well in the yard, but when they were ready to ship, the fat market was down and he stood to lose $40 a head.

Well, he was really mad now. After all the work he'd put into those cattle, he wasn't about to lose that kind of money on them. So he talked to his banker, borrowed a bunch of money, and bought himself a little packing house.

He'd just butcher his own stuff, and to heck with operating at a loss.

Well, he had labor trouble. One of the coolers broke down. The Health Department found evidence that blood was being shed in the killing room. And there was a truckers' strike.

By the time he got his beef sold to the supermarkets, he'd managed to lose $55 a head. He wanted to go ahead and buy a supermarket and roll the dice one more time, but by then his banker had lost his nerve. He'd had about all the vertical integration he could stand.

"What does a man have to do to make money in this business?" Lonnie screamed to the banker.

The old gentleman thought about it for a minute. "Lonnie, I think if you'd stayed drunk for two years and never bought that first cow, you'd have been money ahead."

Which just goes to prove that if a cowboy works hard, culls deep, and watches the market, by the time he's fifty, he'll be old enough to know better.

But Lonnie didn't give up. He was determined to make a living on his ranch, and if anybody can find a way, he will.

I talked to him last week and I think he's coming up with some good ideas. It could be that some of the rest of us might ought to follow his lead.

The first thing he did was to sell every hoof and head on the place. With the cattle gone, that left more grass for the prairie dogs. He's got a contract to sell prairie dogs to a string of zoos in the East.

G.L. Holmes

The next thing he did was to hire a research chemist as a consultant. The chemist's job was to invent products made from natural resources on the ranch. He came up with a kind of fiber-board made from pressed sagebrush and sand burs, and they're going to use it for making *coffins*. They're going to call them Lite Coffins.

I thought that was clever.

But I saved the best one for last. That chemist must have been a genius. He figured out a way of making whiskey out of tumbleweeds!

Now, that's better than spinning straw into gold. To get straw, you have to plant something and irrigate it. Tumbleweeds will grow out of cement.

Besides that, I'd rather own shares in a whiskey factory than find a pot of gold at the end of a rainbow, because it's liable to quit raining before people stop drinking.

I'm betting that it's only a matter of time until Lonnie becomes a wealthy rancher. But he's been snakebit before, and just in case things don't work out, he's applied for food stamps.